I0608145

WHEN CURSE COMES TO LOVE

MAGICAL MIDWAY PARANORMAL COZY SERIES, BOOK #8

LEANNE LEEDS

BADCHEN PUBLISHING

When Curse Comes to Love
Published by Badchen Publishing
14125 W State Highway 29
Suite B-203 119
Liberty Hill, TX 78642 USA

Copyright © 2020 by Leanne Leeds

All rights reserved.

No part of this book may be reproduced in any form or by any electronic or mechanical means, including information storage and retrieval systems, without written permission from the author, except for the use of brief quotations in a book review.

For permissions contact: info@badchenpublishing.com

WHEN CURSE COMES TO LOVE

CHAPTER 1

"PLEASE, JUST STOP!" I SHRIEKED AS LOUD AS I could over the deafening magical force that felt like it was vibrating my very bones. The attack—merciless, unrelenting attack—came from all sides, from all angles, driven by a magic I had never come across before.

It was terrifying.

"Point of order!" Bart Billingsworth, one of the wereducks, quacked as his wife, Bonnie, thrashed her wings aggressively. "The ringmaster is suffering a nervous breakdown!"

"Well, of course she is, you're *honking* at her!" Leo, a werelion, roared.

"*Our* ringmaster looks perfectly fine!" Bubba McAfee, a werelion from the Makepeace Circus, told Leo. "Maybe we should be in charge of this merger! Clearly, Gunther's better at this! He's not howling like a banshee!"

I looked across the long, long, long table at Gunther. My boyfriend—er, husband—was not, in fact, howling like a banshee. He did, however, look like he was dealing with some state of shock considering the perspiration on his brow and the paleness of his face. Catching my eye, he half-smiled, and suddenly leaned his head wearily on his hand.

Gunther and I were presiding over the third meeting of the Magical Midway and the Makepeace Circus. Since accidentally joining the two circuses (and accidentally getting married in the middle of a disaster as opposed to, say, purposefully getting married on a shore in Hawaii like I'd always wanted) Gunther and I had been harangued day after day, night after night, with the demands of our respective citizens.

No ringmasters had ever sought to join two circuses.

Gunther and I were now *very clear* as to why that was.

"Their lion area is *ludicrous*!" Leo shouted, smashing his hand on the table. "I won't have my people living in apartments instead of a den! It's absurd!"

"You live like animals," Bubba snapped.

"We *are* animals!" Leo yelled. "We're lions, you moron! Lions don't have log cabins or tiny houses! We're not some bourgeoisie pride putting on airs—"

"Ah! There! There! Pride! Do you even know what that word means, barn cat?"

"Barn cat! Why I oughta—"

"ENOUGH!" Gunther roared. He hopped out of his chair and glared down everyone at the table. "You're all fighting like children! The next person who talks will lose their voice for a day! I have lost all endurance! You are driving Charlotte and me mad!"

"It's clear we can't all decide this collectively," I agreed with Gunther wearily. "Every time we try, it devolves into squabbling over petty issues, and nothing gets solved."

"Then tell us what to do!" a goblin shouted.

"Be thankful that the threat of the Witches' Council has been removed," Gunther said, his voice returning to normal. "Be grateful that the human has ended the war—"

"She still has a wish!" a leprechaun shouted.

"Yeah, Red is right, she could slaughter us all in an instant!"

"What are you going to do about it?"

The clamor struggled to return to previous ear-splitting levels. I held up my hand, quietly, as Gunther and I gazed at one another across the table. One by one, the voices lowered, and then stopped.

"Go, all of you," I exhaled. "Go back to your current homes, talk amongst yourselves. Decide what you value. Make a list of the things you don't like. Gunther and I will come to each species, each group, together."

"Together, we will find the way forward," Gunther finished.

It took a full ten minutes for everyone to empty out of the room Gunther and I had manifested especially for this merging. We wanted everyone to be a part of it, everyone to have a voice. We didn't want to be like the Witches' Council, dictators telling everybody what the way forward was.

And yet, after weeks, we were stuck.

And we knew it.

∿

"Come here," Gunther said, holding out his arms. I walked over to the couch in our bedroom and gingerly crawled into his embrace. "You looked like you needed a hug," he said. We clunked together.

The clunk riled me up again.

"This is ridiculous!" I pushed him away. "Isn't there supposed to be some kind of reward for people who save the world? We have two hundred paranormals furious at us, two cats at each other's throats, and we're married. Married! But we still can't…we can't…" I fluttered my arms around.

"We can't be with one another as husband and wife," Gunther finished. His face remained serene, but I knew that his calm was primarily for me. I could feel his pain.

"*Be* with one another? Gunther, I'd settle for knowing what your skin feels like at this point!"

Just as I finished, two black cats tumbled into the room, fur flying, claws out.

I told you that was mine!

I'll rip your throat out and eat your entrails for dinner!

Never touch that again! Do you hear me?

Hear you? I can't get you to shut up, you old—

"Please!" Gunther shouted at them.

The cats froze, limbs wrapped around one another, teeth half-sunk into each other's necks. Bright eyes moved from my face to Gunther's, and suddenly they elegantly disentangled and casually moved apart as if nothing had happened.

"I think I've heard you shout more in the last three weeks than I've heard you raise your voice the entire time I've known you," I told Gunther. I sat down on the couch and watched the cats (now studiously avoiding acknowledging either of us).

"Well, honestly, Charlotte, these are the times that try a man's patience," he smiled at me. "I apologize for raising my voice. You're right, it's not like me."

"*None* of this is like us," I said.

"Oh, quit your complaining," Ms. Elkins walked in, Devana on her arm. "You vanquished the Witches' Council. Well, your little human friend beat the Witches' Council," she corrected herself. Devana helped her lower herself to the couch. "But it achieved what you were supposed to do."

"If this is winning, maybe it would have been—"

"Don't you even think about finishing that statement," Ms. Elkins snapped at me, slamming a hand over my mouth. "You won. Enjoy it."

"I won. Right," I sighed.

I arrived at my own pinnacle. I released the paranormal world. I did something accidentally that made it so Gunther and I could be together. In doing so, my friend got her parents back, and a bad person became a good person. The Witches' Council couldn't hurt anyone anymore without harming themselves. If all these things were *good*, why were Gunther and I so miserable?

"So, if I had to guess? You're not done," my mother said. She passed me a slice of Costco pizza. I had teleported down to my parents' from Maggie's in-between paranormal park in the sky. It was an alternate universe of some kind, a hiding place for the circuses that no one else could get to.

While Gunther and I were working things out, we'd just left them there. It seemed easier.

I leaned over and inhaled the cheesy, steaming slice and, like high-fat aromatherapy, it made me feel a little better.

"Sure, what Tabitha wished for got things mostly finished, at least between you and the Witches' Council."

"But it wasn't between us and the Witches' Council," Gunther told my mom, understanding dawning across his face. "Well, it *was*, but it wasn't. Not at its foundation."

"Just because the other side doesn't have a sufficient army anymore doesn't mean the general took his ball and went home," my mother explained and gave Gunther a slice. "The opposition between the two powers still exists. The impasse will persist unless it's ended."

"How do you know?" I asked Mom.

She came over and flicked her nail against my arm, and then Gunther's arm. The metal clinks echoed in Mom's kitchen. "The two of you are supposedly married, and you can't touch one another. Now, maybe I've been living in the human world for a little too long, but that seems to me to be a pretty obvious metaphor."

"You think that's why everyone is arguing?" I asked Gunther.

"Because Maggie and Eiggam are still fighting?" Gunther asked. I nodded. "It's possible, I guess. The Witches' Council can't influence anything anymore, not without some serious repercussions, but..."

"But what?"

"Are the Witches' Council still Eiggam's champions?" Gunther asked.

"No," Mercy World walked into the kitchen, Roland and Gerda Makepeace slipping in behind her. "Eiggam has rescinded his favor from Mina and the Witches' Council. Whatever superpower Mina had? That's gone. She's just a plain huntress witch now, though that's still a formidable creature. Don't misread me."

"Gunther, son, we need to talk to you." Roland glanced over at me. "Alone."

"Dad, anything you have to say to me you can say in front of my wife." Gunther reached across the table and clutched my greasy, cheesy hand. "No secrets."

"Gunther, darling, your father isn't trying to *exclude* Charlotte, honestly." Gerda laid a luminous hand on his shoulder and smiled kindly at me. "We just feel like it might be best if we talk to you about this situation alone first. Then, of course, we can discuss it with Charlotte. Once you've had time to process."

"No secrets," Gunther insisted again. I tried to pull my hand away, but he held it fast. Turning to me, he frowned. "Don't do that. No secrets. We do things *together*."

Mercy turned to Gerda and raised an eyebrow.

"Just tell the boy." Roland waved his hands in the air.

"Eiggam has chosen a new champion. In fact, he chose several weeks ago. With his power withdrawn from us, it took me a while to get here." Mercy rolled her eyes. "Mina and Mabel weren't pleased, as you can guess."

Gunther's hand grasped mine more rigidly.

I studied my husband, but he was gawking at Mercy. His face was pale.

"That's not possible," Gunther told her.

"If you think about it, actually, it's the most obvious thing he could have done." Mercy smiled sadly. "You are both Thirteenth Witches, after all. And now you're perfectly positioned to fight this out. At least from their perspective."

"No," I deadpanned.

"Your husband is now Eiggam's champion," Mercy said, giving words to the worst fear I didn't even realize I had. "You remain Maggie's. It is up to the two of you to work out who will triumph."

"No," I told her again.

"Then the standoff will continue." Mercy shrugged as if she didn't have a care in the world.

"Realize, however, that energy will pervade both of your circuses. They will remain joined but separated. You will remain enclosed in your protections from one another. You will have no children. You will govern over warring factions until your deaths." She paused and looked deeply into my eyes. "If you are so lucky as to still have the means of dying."

"No," I said again.

"Denial accomplishes nothing," Mercy told me coldly.

I pulled my hand away from Gunther and shoved past Mercy and my mother. Once I crashed through the back door I headed, sobbing, toward the kennels.

Denial may accomplish nothing, but acceptance would come a lot easier if I was cuddling a puppy.

CHAPTER 2

"CHARLOTTE! CHARLOTTE, ARE YOU IN HERE?"

It was my father's voice. Why he even bothered to call out, I don't even know. It was just ten seconds later that he glanced into the stall. "Traitor," I fussed at the schnauzer puppy happily gnawing on my knuckle.

"It wasn't him, actually," my dad replied. He dropped down on the floor next to me and scratched the puppy behind the ears. "You should know by now that he who passes out the food is the alpha."

"That's not true," I grumbled.

"You're right, there's more to it than that. Isn't there always more to things than we think, Charlotte?" Dad asked, his eyes sympathetic.

"Come on, talk to me, honey. We've barely spoken since all this started, really."

"You didn't want me involved with the paranormal world or the circuses when I was growing up." I put the puppy down. "Did you know this could happen? Was that why?"

Dad looked puzzled. "What do you mean by *this?*"

"I don't even know anymore," I sighed, and I put my head down on my knees. "I just wonder if I would have been better prepared for all this if I'd known what could happen. If you'd let me—"

"Now, look, Charlotte—Gunther was raised as a proper witch," Dad pointed out (even though he rolled his eyes when he said the term *proper*). "I don't see that he's dealing with this all that much better than you are, honey."

"How am I supposed to fix two gods being mad at each other? Two *married* gods? When I'm not even a *proper* witch?"

"Stop that. You're missing something," Dad told me, his head tilting.

"I'm *always* missing something. And *why* isn't Ms. Elkins helping me anymore?" I asked him, smacking my head against the wall lightly, but hard enough that it made a heavy clank. "She insisted this was all fixed."

"From what you've said, even when she was helping you, she wasn't *really* helping you," Dad pointed out mildly. The puppy barked. "You've gotten this far, Charlotte. You did that, not Ms. Elkins. You, and Gunther, and your friends."

"That's true," I murmured.

"If that's been the case, I don't think you will solve anything sitting alone out here with a puppy," Dad smiled

I hated how calm Dad always was about everything. Twenty dogs from a hoarder's house? No problem. The sheriff harassing us again? No problem. Mafia princess murdered in the kennel? No problem. Everything that shook my Dad's world, he just shook with it so everything vibrated at the same level and all was well.

"Did you *want* to be the ringmaster?" I challenged him. His eyes met mine, and he raised his eyebrow. "I mean, I don't think we ever talked about it, not really. I never really asked you how you felt not being chosen. Did it bother you?"

"I wouldn't say that it bothered me, Charlotte," Dad glanced around the kennel. "Your mother and I like our life here, and I wouldn't have wanted to leave it."

"But?"

"No one wants their child to suffer,

Charlotte." He reached out and put his arm
around my shoulder. "You're my only daughter,
and I love you dearly. This is a hard gig, and I
knew that. I hoped that your Uncle Phil would
stay the ringmaster until long after you and I
were dead and buried. He loved the circus."

"He still does," I told Dad. Dad grinned.

"I mean when he was alive, he loved the circus,
and he loved being the ringmaster. Phil was born
for this, always wanted it, and it was a
ridiculously silly accident that poisoned him."
Dad dropped the smile and frowned. "Or maybe
it wasn't a mishap. Maybe you and Gunther were
meant to be the ringmasters at this time all along."

"That's what Ethel Elkins says," I told him.

"She also says everything's fixed," Dad pointed
out. "If you and your new husband are the
champions of an estranged supernatural power
couple and their opposite plans, I have to say I
suspect she *may* be incorrect on that count."

"Why does she say everything's fixed?" I
mused. Scrambling up off the floor, I turned and
extended a hand to my father. The puppy yelped
in disappointment. Within seconds, the young
dog's mother trotted around the corner and
nosed him back to his siblings. "I guess there's

only one way to find out," I told Dad as I jerked him up to his feet.

~

"Because I told you from the beginning my job was to keep the Witches' Council from doing terrible things to people using superpowers they shouldn't have. That's *done*," Ethel Elkins snapped. "How many times do you want me to restate this?"

"There's no way everything can be fixed if Eiggam and Maggie are still fighting. You told me that the whole point of all this was to keep one person from winning."

"I did not."

"You did, though."

"Well, if I did, I had no idea that your human person would intervene and wish all the abuses in the paranormal world away with a snap of her fingers." Ms. Elkins squinted and shoved her glasses back up on her nose. "Could you have foreseen that? I couldn't have foreseen that. And if *I* couldn't have foreseen it, *no one* could have foreseen it."

"This was about *more* than my mother,"

Devana said, moving closer to Ms. Elkins perch on the edge of the couch.

"Was it, though? Was it, really?" the old woman said in a tiresome voice, tilting her head. "I don't think you children truly grasped what was going on here."

"That's because *you* were the person in charge of telling us what was going on here!" I exclaimed.

"Well, since that hasn't changed, I'm telling you you're done." Ms. Elkins reached into her bag and pulled out yarn and knitting needles. "What do you want, extra credit? More excitement? Just sit back, run your circus, enjoy your life."

"I want to kiss my boyfriend without it sounding like two lead pipes slamming together! I want to join our circuses without everyone feeling like they want to kill everyone else!"

"I want to make my last wish," Tabitha said softly from the corner as she hiked up the genie lamp. "I'm holding on to it, though, because I suspect you're not quite being truthful with Charlotte."

"Save the world once and they get overconfident." Ms. Elkins mumbled as she began knitting. "I'm being as sincere as I'm capable of being, young lady."

"Yeah, that's not really making me feel better, here," Tabitha told her.

"So," Gunther said as he strode into the yurt. "I have some news, and I'm sure no one will like it." Turning to me, he softened his voice. "Are you all right?"

"Sure, why wouldn't I be?" I deadpanned. Gunther caught my hand in his and squeezed. I squeezed back and gave him a sad little smile. "I'm handling. What have you got?"

"This room, the people in this room, are likely the only ones not affected by the power," Gunther explained as he gestured for us to sit down. The only people in the room were Gunther and me, Devana and Ms. Elkins, and Tabitha. "It's conceivable that Aidan and Kyle are fine, too, since they're half-human and not here."

"I'm all right." Fortuna dashed into the yurt and closed the door decisively behind her. "I felt that shift in intensity, though."

"What shift?" I asked, mystified.

"I spoke to Eiggam," Gunther explained. "I was over on the Makepeace Circus side of the joined circuses, and that was evidently all he needed."

"All he needed for what?"

"To take over the Makepeace Circus, girl. Haven't you been paying attention to anything that's going on?" Ms. Elkins asked me with annoyance. "What did you think it meant when Mercy claimed that Gunther had been chosen?"

"Wait, do you mean—"

"Maggie is the energy animating and protecting the Magical Midway," Gunther told me. "But now Eiggam is the energy animating and securing the Makepeace Circus."

"Our circuses don't share the same energy anymore?" I asked Gunther. He shook his head no. "But what does that mean?"

The normal low hum of conversation that played in the yurt's background at all times had picked up in volume. Shouts now punctuated it. Then a crash.

"So, the two circuses are fighting," Fortuna said, her hands slightly shaking as she worked them nervously in front of her. "Everyone from our circus is mad at everybody from their circus. They don't know why, they are just—"

"You have to be kidding me," I told her. I pushed up and sidestepped the coffee table. "What are they fighting about?"

"Everything. Nothing," Fortuna explained, stepping back. "I think because I was once fully human, I am not being affected by this energy that seems to have invaded everything. I can't be sure."

"I feel fine," Tabitha shrugged.

Gunther and I stepped out onto the Magical Midway.

Where all hell had broken loose.

CHAPTER 3

THE INHABITANTS OF THE MAGICAL MIDWAY WERE streaming in twos and threes toward the Makepeace Circus. Some of them carried honest-to-goodness pitchforks, and they were pumping them toward Gunther's circus.

"Let's get them!"

"Take that tunnel down!"

"You grab the right flank!"

"Protect the children! Those gargoyles *eat* children!"

"The gargoyles don't eat *children*, do they?" I yelled toward Gunther. Gunther shouted back that they did not, and it provided me a split second of relief before the marching carnie hordes stopped and spun to gawk at Gunther Makepeace. Fury sparked from their eyes.

"What are *you* doing here? Traitor!"

"Get him!"

"Kill him!"

"We can't *kill* him, he's a ringmaster!"

"Well, bang on him! Loudly! Maybe the sound will give him a headache!"

They hadn't even reached him, and the sound was already giving *me* a headache.

"Back off, all of you!" I ordered them, and the progress of the Magical Midway possessed horde stopped instantaneously. "No one will attack Gunther, do you hear me? No one will attack anyone." They glared back at me, at least a hundred eyes, in annoyance. "Why are you all suddenly so angry?"

"He's the enemy!"

"The conspirators are attached to our circus!"

"We have to protect ourselves! We have to defend the children!"

"There are, like, *maybe* ten children in the entire circus," I told them. I crossed my arms. "I don't know why so few of you have kids, but other than the goblins, there are almost no kids here. You can relax."

"I don't mean you, or your children, any

harm." Gunther stepped forward, his arms wide. Fifty or more paranormals gasped and stepped back, staring at him cautiously. "You all know me. I've lived here with you before. I would harm none of you."

"You're a liar!" someone shouted angrily from the back of the crowd. My eyes traveled over the group trying to spot who had just called Gunther a liar, but I couldn't. The angry expressions that played across the faces of so many people I'd come to know showed it could have been any one of them. They were infused with a fury I had rarely seen in anyone other than the Witches' Council.

"Go home," I stepped forward and told them all. "Go back to your yurts. I apologize to all of you that you feel this way, because you shouldn't."

"We want that circus away from us!"

"They shouldn't be joined! He shouldn't be here!"

"We will never, ever be part of the Makepeace Circus!"

"Go back to your yurts now!" I roared, and they trembled away from me. Despite everything that had happened, although we had grown comfortable with one another through many trials and tribulations? I was still the ringmaster. Technically, this was still an autocracy, and when I told people to return to their yurts...

They went.

Okay, admittedly, it might've been the red haze of energy that I glowed with because I was so ticked off. That might've scared them a little.

Gunther and I stood in front of my yurt and watched as people resentfully dispersed, protesting under their breath. Slowly, the road in front of my home emptied.

Until a crash from the Makepeace Circus cut through the silence.

~

"You will no come here, you stupid dumb Roman!" At the midpoint of the circus attachment tunnel, Ambom roared at Bob, his weapon poised and ready to stab the angry lares guard. "You want you people? We throw them to you! You like play catch? You catch wereduck!"

Irum, another gargoyle, stood beside Ambom holding a petrified, quacking duck. "We no throw back. We eat duck?" he asked his brother. "I think we eat duck."

"You will *not* eat that wereduck," Gunther said.

We both walked into the tunnel connecting our two circuses. "Give me the duck, Irum."

Irum tossed the terrified duck to Gunther and shrugged. "We have were-elephant, too. We eat him."

"You will not eat any of the were-animals at all. Not from our circus, not from their circus. Not even if they don't belong to a circus," Gunther told the gargoyles. He gripped the duck close and petted it consolingly in an attempt to calm it down.

The duck turned on Gunther and began thrashing his chest with its bill. The clangs made the tunnel sound like a harbor during fishing season.

"I've got him," I said as I snatched the duck to our side of the tunnel. With a snuggle and a last quack in Gunther's direction, the duck jumped down and toddled off at breakneck speed.

"I should kill you for that," Bob told the gargoyle, his face as impassively sociopathic as I'd ever seen it. "You and your brother both. Take a step across, gargoyle. See what happens."

"Stop it," I told Bob and stepped in front of him. Gunther and I took up positions on either side of the imaginary line between the two circuses. An imaginary line that, while still not visible, had just become far more palpable. "Don't goad them. We don't want anyone to get hurt here."

"Stupid lady ringmaster," Ambom said, underlining the comment with something that sounded like a laugh, but considering it was a gargoyle and he was made of stone, I couldn't really be sure. "We gargoyles. We no get hurt. Roman flesh and bone. Roman get *dead*."

Irum snorted. I think.

"You will *not* talk to my wife like that," Gunther told the gargoyle.

That still completely freaked me out. I knew this wasn't the time, or the place, to contemplate that. But hearing Gunther call me his wife? It was unsettling, each and every time.

"Don't care. Still stupid lady ringmaster," Ambom told him. "Shouldn't be wife. Shouldn't be here. Should be far away."

"I told you," a voice thundered from the Makepeace Circus side of the tunnel. "We have spent hundreds of years apart. Our energy can no longer mix. Move the circus, Champion."

"What is that?" I gasped as a light gleamed brightly.

"That's Eiggam," Gunther sighed.

We sent the guards away. It took some doing, sending them back into the circus. Bob hadn't regressed to the monosyllabic communication methods of his brothers, but his disposition was more serious than I had ever seen it. Finally, though, it was just Gunther and me and the light at the end of the tunnel.

You know the old joke about the approaching train?

Yeah.

"It is appropriate that you take this circus and move it away from hers," Eiggam told Gunther, the light flowing in circles as it seemed to draw the form of a man with lasers. "It will soothe the resentment of our citizens."

"They aren't *our* citizens, Eiggam."

"They have *always* been our citizens," the glowing faceless form responded. "It is this time and this place and this way of things that will be the new, always. And so it has always been this way because that is what *I* say."

"Holy crap, I thought *mine* was difficult to understand," I murmured to Gunther. "What is he even—"

"I do not wish to cause our citizens any more

pain," Eiggam said, cutting me off. "But if you continue this lunacy of linking your circus to the other one, your citizens will continue to feel fury at the Magical Midway's proximity."

"I didn't ask for this," Gunther said.

"I am not in the habit of waiting for invitations," Eiggam responded.

"Why are you and Maggie so angry at one another?" I asked the specter. He went on talking to Gunther as if I hadn't said a word.

"Move the circus," Eiggam demanded.

"Is he ignoring me?" I asked Gunther.

"He can't *see* you," Gunther murmured.

"Who are you talking to?" Eiggam asked as he began walking toward the two of us. "Who else is here? Tell me, I demand to know."

Gunther shook his head no. "I'm not going to tell you anything."

"Then perhaps I have chosen poorly."

"Perhaps you have," Gunther told the godlike being through clenched teeth. "Again, I remind you, I *didn't* ask for this."

"We are in *her* place," Eiggam told Gunther. "I do not wish to be here anymore. I want to be away from that woman's energy. Move the circus."

"No," Gunther responded.

"I can take you over. I can *make* you do what I want," Eiggam informed Gunther as he sauntered, step-by-step, towards the center of the tunnel. "You are utterly under my control."

"Ah, yeah, so, I don't think that's *really* true," Gunther said, putting his arm around me. "See, I think if that *was* true, *you* would still have control of the Witches' Council. Or, at the very least, my circus would've already been moved."

Eiggam stared at Gunther.

"Since you renounced your alliance with the Witches' Council because Mina's pretty much useless now, and since the Makepeace Circus is sitting in the middle of Maggie's little garden right next to the Magical Midway, and it doesn't look to be going anywhere unless I move it, I have a hypothesis. You want to hear it?"

"I can't wait," Eiggam growled.

"Yeah, me neither," I said.

"I think you and Maggie can choose who holds your power, but all that stuff we were told about you guys *letting* us do this, that, and the other?" Gunther said. My husband was looking at Eiggam as if he was sizing him up. "I don't think *you* let us do anything. I think you handed your power over to us."

"Do you, now?" Eiggam placed his hands on his…hips? I think hips. Probably hips.

"I do. I think Charlotte and I have your power."

"I can just take it from you. The way I did from Mina," Eiggam sneered. "And if you continue challenging me, I will."

"Yeah, about that," Gunther said, stepping away from me. "Why don't you try?"

"Here?"

"Sure."

"Right now?"

"No time like the present." Gunther smiled and held his arms out. "I'm right here. I'm not the champion you wanted, so why not just take the power you gave me and go give it to someone else? Maybe the gargoyles."

"I…I don't want to…" Eiggam shot Gunther a look that could have left my new husband a pile of ash on the floor if there was any energy behind it.

"You don't want to?"

"No."

"Or you can't."

"I could if I wanted to. I just don't want to."

"I don't understand what's going on here," I told Gunther, blinking furiously as I tried to process what was happening. "Why are you playing chicken with a superpowered being?"

"Because he's not a superpowered being," Gunther told me. Turning to me, he looked me in the eye and smiled. "I am. You are. But he's not."

"Of course he is! He's the power that animates you, so…"

"We are both ringmasters, Charlotte."

"Right. I got that part."

"How do we lose our power? How did Maggie ensure that ringmasters could defend themselves against attacks from the Witches' Council?"

"She made us…immortal. Unkillable," I answered, the full import of the miscalculation that Eiggam made suddenly dawning on me. "And our power is almost—"

"Impossible to steal," Gunther said, nodding. "But he can't see you, and the two of them can't see each other. So Eiggam didn't realize that when he gave me his power—"

"He *can't take it back*," I gasped. "Because you're still a ringmaster, and that's something *Maggie* did."

"Not him," Gunther nodded.

"Not me what?" Eiggam asked angrily. "Tell me!"

Gunther waved away the god-like being of

light like he was an annoying fly. Smiling at me, Gunther shrugged. "You ready to sort out the world?"

"That's…terrifying…" I whispered as we hugged with a clank. "Aargh! Can we actually remove this stupid metal armor ourselves? Do you *really* think—"

"Absolutely. Let's," Gunther smiled, and grabbed my hands.

I had only a *second* to marvel at the soft touch of Gunther's hands before the two of us flew back from one another as if we had wrapped our hands around live wires.

CHAPTER 4

"WE TOUCH EACH OTHER, THE ENERGY BLOWS US apart," Gunther explained to Fortuna once we were back in my yurt. "So, we managed to remove our armor together—"

"But now instead of clanking, we explode," I finished.

"That's not good." Fortuna shook her head.

"Have you been able to find anyone else unaffected by the energy that these two demons let loose?"

Fortuna's face went white. "We have *demons* now?"

"I think she's referring to Maggie and Eiggam," Tabitha told her. Fortuna looked at her, eyes wide, and nodded.

"How *dare* you call me a demon," a voice shrieked from the corner of the room. Light swirled again, just like it had in the tunnel, and a version of Maggie appeared. Regal, elegant, with a silver crown atop her head. "I am no demon. Really. A demon," Maggie scoffed.

"What do *you* want?" I asked Maggie coldly. Without the armor, my body felt…strange. As if the weariness from everything I'd been through had been captured, filtered by the invisible armor that encased me. Without it, I was tired.

"To put your armor back on you," Maggie said with a toss of her head. "You don't want to get stabbed by one of the Makepeace Circus people, do you? Mauled by a wildcat? Torn limb from limb by a bear? You are utterly unprotected," Maggie told me as she lifted her hand, a metal ball of goo sloshing above her palm.

"Stop," I told her, stepping back.

"Don't be daft. Let me restore the armor—"

"I mean it, Maggie. Stop."

"Charlotte, maybe we didn't think this through," Gunther said, looking at Maggie. "She's right, with everyone's rage hyped up artificially by whatever the two of them are doing, we're vulnerable. Both of us."

"Not if we create our own shielding," I told

him. "We have their powers, right? Whatever *she* can do, *I* can do if you're right about what's going on. And I can do it better."

"Balderdash!" Maggie exclaimed. Her eyes sparked with…I don't know. Something. "I am older than you and better than you. I was *constructed* that way!"

"Oh, just back yourself up there, lady," I barked. I turned away from her and looked at Gunther. "Let's say that you're right. Let's say that they gave us all of their powers. If that's the case, what's stopping us from undoing the limitations they've placed on us?"

"Well, you don't know that the limitations on you are from *them*, for one," Tabitha pointed out. "They don't handle all the witch rules, do they? I mean, *some* of these things are probably from them, sure. You have to have the equivalent of, like, magic physics or something, don't you?"

"I don't know, do we?" I asked Gunther.

"Tabitha's right, there are fundamental rules concerning how magic, all magic, works," Gunther said. He raked his fingers through his hair. "The thing is, we break those rules. What Charlotte and I can do as ringmasters isn't really supposed to be *done*."

"What's the explanation for the ringmasters?" Fortuna asked.

"That higher-level beings created them; the same for the lawgivers. I guess you'd call it a theological explanation?" Gunther shrugged. "There are origin stories to the things that operate outside of expected parameters."

"See? There you go. I'm a deity. So you better do what I'm telling you," Maggie demanded with a flash of exasperation.

"Before we try anything else, I think we have to move both of the circuses back down to earth," I told them. A fresh swell of annoyance tightened my chest. "We really are in uncharted territory here, and I don't want to poke around the magical limitations while we're suspended in a substitute universe."

"That's a good idea," Gunther said. "My only concern is putting hundreds of enraged carnies back in Mickwac."

"So, you have some kind of big magic dome thing that protects people from the outside around the circuses, right? Can you change that thing so it keeps everybody *in*?" Tabitha asked.

"I don't know." I spun to Gunther. He shrugged his shoulders. "I guess we could try it, but again, I don't think it's a good idea to try anything else here. We don't want to get stuck here."

"We will have to do it almost as soon as we touch down." Gunther raised his chin and looked toward the door. "Once we do that, the circuses will be wholly detached."

"You two will still be able to leave, though, right?"

"They can't answer that because they both have no idea what they're doing," Maggie murmured and brushed her palms together. "They are like babes in the woods, floundering through things they don't understand."

"At some point, we have to make a leap of faith," I called over to her.

"Faith in *what*, exactly?"

"Ourselves," I responded.

The glittering white goddess had no reply.

"That's it," I breathed. The trees surrounding my parents' house leaped into view, and my skin felt the cool Texas evening air. "Here we go."

I closed my eyes and imagined turning the dome inside out. Pictured my own people standing at the borders of the Magical Midway unable to get out.

"I think it's done," I breathed again. "Can you test it?"

Fortuna walked several steps forward, her arms outstretched to ensure that she didn't injure herself. On the ninth step her hand came in contact with...something. "Oh, gross, Charlotte, it's wet! It's wet and spongy, like goo. Oh, this is just disgusting," she complained.

"I want to feel," Tabitha said. She stepped over to Fortuna and reached her hand out. "Weird. I don't feel anything." With a few more steps, she was outside the borders of the Magical Midway. "Am I supposed to be able to do this? I left the circus, right? I'm not supposed to be out here, am I?"

"She's human, you *idiots*," Maggie said, drifting toward us. "You didn't bind her to the circus, and she's human. You can't contain her."

Tabitha jumped as the Makepeace Circus whomped down two feet from where she stood. The entire fairgrounds glowed for a split second and then ceased.

"He wouldn't have crushed you," I told her as I walked forward, my hands feeling for the unseen wall. With a few more steps, I wandered past

Fortuna and was standing next to Tabitha on the outside of the Magical Midway. "There's some automatic something or another that keeps the circuses from squashing humans that get in the way."

"The way that all of this magic stuff works exactly as expected, Charlotte, *really* makes that statement super comforting," my friend informed me sarcastically.

"There is Gunther," Fortuna said, pushing against the goo. "I think what you did is adequate, Charlotte. No matter how hard I push I cannot accompany you and Tabitha."

"Good, there's one thing taken care of. At least everyone is protected while we figure all this out."

"What is there to figure out?" Maggie asked as she started toward me. Raising her chin, she stepped past Fortuna only to be met by a sucking sound that reverberated across the field. The beautiful goddess's face became distorted as if we smashed her against a window. With an echoing boing, she bounced back next to Fortuna. "What fresh perdition is *this*? Charlotte Astley, *what* have you done?"

As Maggie was shrieking at me, Gunther stepped out into the in-between safe zone, the strip of land between the two circuses that neither Maggie nor Eiggam controlled. With a clang, Eiggam bounced back into the Makepeace Circus.

"Did you lock him in there, too?" I asked him, my eyes wide.

"I didn't mean to. Is he *sealed* in there?" Gunther asked, spinning in astonishment to watch Eiggam bang against the wall he had flipped to hold the Makepeace inhabitants. "Wait, Maggie's locked in the Magical Midway?"

"You two would be especially impressive if you had a single clue about what you were doing," Tabitha observed.

"You didn't do it on purpose?" Gunther asked me. I shook my head no. "Me neither."

"They *are* paranormal," I suggested. The three of us regarded the two gods while they slowly recognized that we had confined them in the circuses they wielded against one another. "I suppose both of us were just vague enough to pull off something that we didn't even know we could do!"

"*Wait* until I get out of here," Maggie said ominously, quivering with rage. "You will rue the day that you ever *met* me, Ringmaster."

"I got news for you, lady," I told her as she continued to shudder with fury. "I already do."

"So, now everyone's locked into the circus except for the two of us and Tabitha, it seems like we have more powers than we originally assumed, but since the powers are so potent and yet so undefined…" I trailed off and glanced at Gunther.

"We are not altog*ether* certain what our next move is," Gunther explained to my parents. We sat on the deck staring out over the two circuses. Tabitha had returned to the Magical Midway to check on Bob. "We want to settle this once and for all, obviously, but we're also afraid that we don't understand the influence that we hold."

"That you're thinking about those things at all, Gunther, is a positive thing," my mother informed him as she patted his hand. "I'm not sure that Alan and I will be much help, though. You two really are navigating a situation that the paranormal world has never seen before."

"And for good reason," my father added. "I've always believed that the ringmaster power was too much for anyone being to have. It's just not right."

"Now, Alan, let's not start that again—"

"Martha, don't tsk-tsk me," Dad interrupted and pointed at Mom.

"Alan, darling, unless you'd like to surrender that finger, I recommend you point it somewhere else," Mom cooed at him warmly. Dad's face relaxed and his hand came to settle back in his lap. "Much better, dear."

Considering everything that had been going on, what Mom just did suddenly alarmed me. Why was it okay for her to unilaterally change what Dad felt? To stop him from expressing his opinion because the emotions that charged that judgment were, in her view, negative?

"Do you think that was wrong?" I asked Mom. She lifted her eyebrow at me. Despite the caution signs flashing in her eyes, I pushed forward. "I mean, Dad was clearly agitated. You used your power to transform how he *felt*. I'm not trying to make you mad or pass judgment or anything, I'm just curious. Do you think it's ethical?"

"Your father and I are married, dear," Mom said, pulling a piece of lint from Dad's sleeve. "There's a particular entanglement in being joined in marriage, an awareness of the boundaries of intrusion that come from years of living together as a couple. One day, you and Gunther will understand."

"So you wouldn't do that to someone else?"

"I would do it to you, perhaps less so now

that you're an adult," Mom admitted. "But you're my daughter, and I spent years being responsible for you, being responsible for protecting you. I wouldn't use my power as much on Gunther, for example. Unless it was clearly called for because someone would be harmed."

"How do you decide?" I asked her.

"Well, Charlotte, it's just the type of person you are. I hope that I operate with people's best interests at heart, that I've learned enough from experience and mistakes that I've made that I make good choices," Mom said and then leaned forward, clutching the arm of her chair. "Why all the questions suddenly?"

"Gunther was the one that realized that he and I have a tremendous amount of power, a power that no one can take from us. It's clearly a mistake, though—I don't think Maggie or Eiggam realized that they were giving us something that they couldn't take back," I told her. "Since it was a mistake, ethically, we should probably just give it back, right?"

"That's one choice," my father said.

"But it was their mistake and their decisions that started all this, so that doesn't seem like a fantastic option."

"You don't want us to have it, do you?" Gunther asked me softly.

"We just imprisoned *our circuses*, Gunther," I told him, my shoulders slumping. "That's not something I would've ever thought either one of us would do. We imprisoned your mother and father. Your sister. My uncle."

"It was to protect them, though," Gunther pointed out.

"It was to protect them, and the things that are threatening them are only threatening them because of what we are," I reasoned. "We are the ringmasters. We are the champions of two powerful beings. Two powerful, immature, hostile and angry beings."

"That hold two powers, two energies, that the world needs," Gunther said.

"Yeah, well, maybe that's not right, either," I suggested, and my shoulders slumped even further. "And honestly, the world's been doing just fine without them. Maybe they aren't as important anymore as they assume they are."

"I wouldn't tell *them* that," my mother said.

"Maybe someone needs to," I disagreed.

CHAPTER 5

IT WAS DECEPTIVELY QUIET WHEN GUNTHER AND I trudged down the path toward our angry circuses. He didn't speak to me, and I didn't speak to him, not for a while. We were both lost within our own heads, our own thoughts. When we were halfway down the path, Gunther stopped.

"If I had asked you to marry me, would you have done it?"

I paused and turned to him. "What does it matter?" I answered after a pause. "I wasn't asked, and they gave neither of us the choice."

"It *matters.*"

Gunther didn't reach for me, almost as if he wished to give me space to consider the question free of any sway. I appreciated it—Gunther was always considerate that way. Well, almost always.

"Okay, you tell me—why do you think, amid all this, whether I would have said yes matters at all? What's done is done, Gunther."

"Is it, though?" Gunther asked. He lowered his head. His eyes stared somewhere near my feet, and I could see his chest rising and falling with his deep, steady breathing. For a second, I was struck by how elegant he was as the moonlight bathed him in a celestial radiance. "I would have asked you, Charlotte. I would have."

"Yeah, but you didn't," I declared, perhaps a little too firmly.

"No, I didn't," he said. He lifted his face and his vivid blue eyes found mine. "I could tell you it was out of consideration for what you were going through, but that would be a lie. I didn't think you would say yes. I didn't want to be rejected. I was a coward—"

"Gunther, you are anything but a coward!"

"No, don't." He held up his hand. "I *am* a coward when it comes to you. Maybe it's how I grew up. Maybe it was a fear of losing you the way I lost my mother," Gunther said, his face pinching with remembered anguish. "Maybe it was constantly being an outsider in the witch world, the glowing half-witch that didn't deserve to be there and yet would acquire one of the most archaic powers there was. I don't know."

He went on studying me, his eyes tender. As defensive as I felt, he could warm me with a glance. "In any case, I do want to know. Would you have accepted my proposal if I asked you to be my wife, Charlotte?"

Men.

We had two circuses full of paranormals filled with the fury of two ancient, powerful beings. They were detained for their own safety and we had no idea what to do next. But Gunther decided he would recreate the *Do you love me?* scene from *Fiddler on the Roof*.

It suddenly struck me—I'd never heard Gunther sing. I didn't know whether he liked Broadway musicals. What type of books he liked to read. Did he even want kids? I mean, we didn't have that option for a long time, but did he want them? How many?

"Oh, Gunther," I exhaled. His tilted his head, but pain flared in his eyes. "Don't *you* do that. I can see it, you're preparing for me to say that I wouldn't have. But…it's not so straightforward as a yes or a no."

"Then tell me," he replied gently.

"I love you *so* much," I confessed, my eyes unexpectedly filling with tears. I wiped them away hastily. "Had you and I just met, gone on a date, gone to the movies—had we been normal? I believe I'd be doodling *Charlotte Makepeace* on random pieces of paper like a schoolgirl. But nothing about this, nothing about *us*, has been normal."

"I wish it could have been," he whispered. "If that's what you would have wanted, I wish that it could have been."

"Oh, lord, don't wish for something like that, the world may tilt on its axis!" I told him, grinning and crying at the same time. He smiled sadly as I rubbed away more tears that were coming from someplace I couldn't name, couldn't find, and couldn't shove down.

But he still didn't reach for me.

"I would have wanted the choice," I said finally as we stood on either side of the path. "I would have wanted to be asked. To have a surprise proposal, a rose, a ring. An engagement celebration. A wedding. Those are all things I fantasized about as a little girl. But most of all, I expected I would have the *choice*. And I didn't."

"I know."

Of course he knew. Gunther seemed to always know.

"That's really what it comes down to. I love you, Gunther, and I can't imagine ever loving someone else," I told him, lifting my hand toward him. Then I let it drop. "In any other circumstances, at any other time, if it was just you and me? I know becoming your wife would have been the most amazing thing that ever happened to me. I would have said yes."

His eyes glistened with unshed tears. I could feel relief and pain and anger fighting within him. Relief that it was something I wanted, that I loved him. Pain that our *marriage* was something that I felt I had no choice in, and that made me conflicted about it. Anger that it wasn't as perfect as it could have been. And like him, I *knew* it could have been.

"Choice isn't something there's an abundance of in the paranormal world," Gunther told me. "What is that saying in your world? There's always a bigger fish?"

"I wish we could change that," I told him. His head jerked up. "What?"

"Well...*could* we?" he asked me slowly.

"Could we *what*?"

"Change it? Make the playing field more even.

Give people their choices back. The Witches' Council took power because of Eiggam. We have our power because of Maggie. Could we..." he trailed off and stared at me.

"What, *remake* the paranormal world?" I laughed nervously. "Are you being *serious*?"

"Honestly? I don't know," Gunther said, his eyes twinkling as he reached to grab my hand, closing the distance between us. "But it's something to think about."

As soon as he touched my hand, the sound of lightning cracking gave us the split-second warning that we forgot something *really* significant. When I sat up within a bush seconds later, I searched around. Gunther looked down at me from his perch in a tree across the path.

"We're going to need to figure out how to fix that," Gunther called down.

"You think?" I hollered back, picking leaves from my hair.

The madness was like a foggy miasma floating within a snow globe. Faces pressed against the partition between the circuses as each side shouted across the divide at the other side. Even

Samson and Delilah paced, hissing, fur up and tails poofed. Fortuna looked out at me, haggard.

"We have to do something," I told Gunther. "This is all visible if any human comes sauntering in, and this isn't explainable at all."

"It is noticeable," Samantha Goodfellow walked in arm in arm with Tabitha's mother, Sarah Stevens. The two women, both the mothers of Darius Stevens's children, looked for all the world like two best friends. "Do you have *any* idea the spiritual racket you're causing? I was conducting a meditation class at the shop, and *two people* punched one another out!"

"Is my daughter all right?" Sarah asked, looking back and forth at the two angry mobs with a concerned expression.

"Fortuna? Have you seen Tabitha?" I turned and asked.

"I have; she's with Bob," Fortuna nodded. "She's still unaffected by this…well, this."

"What is all this, Charlotte?" The portly priestess captured my arm. "Gunther? Clearly, something is wrong."

"Actually, this is better than it was," I sighed, and revealed to her what had transpired. "Gunther and I are trying to figure out how to fix it, but at the moment? We can't even touch one another."

"Oh, pish posh, of course you can," Samantha gave a dismissive shake of her hand.

"No, we really can't," I told her. I combed my fingers through my hair only to find another leaf. I pulled it out and presented it her. "Gunther and I tend to only be able to fix things that involve both circuses when we touch, when we do things together. When we get near each other, there's a big lightning strike sound and then a jolt that's bright and then we take off in opposite directions."

"All the power in the world, and you still haven't grasped that you can just *use* it, Charlotte." Samantha clutched my hand, and grabbed Gunther's. Standing in between us, she closed her eyes and murmured. "Now, repeat after me."

"Wait a minute—"

"Repeat after me," she said, yanking on our hands. I looked over at Gunther helplessly.

"Is it any dumber than everything else we've done?" he asked me. "We'll hear the words. If they're bad, we just won't say them."

"Sense, fantastic," Samantha told Gunther and yanked again. "Are we ready? Repeat after me.

The boundaries that block us from one another..."

"The boundaries that block us from one another..." Gunther and I said haltingly.

"Are abolished," Samantha said.

"Are abolished," we concluded.

"Nicely done, children," Samantha said as she dropped our hands. "Was that so complicated?"

"That's it?" I asked skeptically.

"What were you expecting? Thunder, lightning, flashes of ghostly light wrapping about you like a serpent? Rose petals showering down from the sky?" Samantha chuckled. "You will it. You say it. It's done."

"Is that how it works for humans?" Gunther asked.

"Well, *we* have to concentrate a bit more and often what we can do is no more than throwing a pebble in a pond," Samantha explained as she grabbed Gunther's hand. "It's about forming intent. For us, it's a step in a process, and it certainly doesn't always work. But *you* two have a tremendous amount of power. For you, I assume it works just that simply."

"May I?" Gunther asked, reaching for my hand.

"Stand back," I cautioned the humans. Taking

a deep breath, I braced, and reached back for Gunther's hand. As his powerful fingers locked around mine, a quiver ran down my spine.

"You okay?" Gunther asked as he strode forward, his eyes alight with faith. I nodded. He reached out with his other hand and his palm caressed my cheek. "You're so soft. Your skin," he stammered. "Charlotte, you are just so incredibly beautiful." His eyes glowed as his hand released mine and he moved slowly to cradle my face in his palms.

I wanted to tell him how handsome he was, how extraordinary he smelled, how protected I felt at his touch, but I couldn't speak.

For a time, we were the only two individuals in the universe. I felt like my insides were disintegrating, and I was humming with elation as his eyes held mine. He leaned down closer, and I closed my eyes. His lips found mine, and I had my very first kiss, true kiss from Gunther.

It was almost too much bliss to experience.

I was so wrapped up in Gunther's kiss (and, holy smoke, that boy could *kiss*) that I scarcely noted the snorts, awwwws, and coos on either side of us.

"That was worth the wait," Gunther whispered. He pecked me on my nose and sought to pull away. I gripped him tighter, sinking my face in his chest and basking in the soft strength of him. "Um, Charlotte?" Gunther whispered.

"Umm hmmm," I murmured without drawing my head up. His arms loosened around me.

"Charlotte," he stated a bit more strongly, and I pulled my head up, concerned. Gunther pointed to the Makepeace Circus and I shifted to look.

Behind the throng of sniffling citizens, Wayland Black held up a placard with writing on it.

Quit farting around! The Galenite Witches are gone!

CHAPTER 6

I COULDN'T PASS INTO THE MAKEPEACE CIRCUS.

Well, I mean, I *could*. Like, I could walk into it. But as soon as I passed over the border, the carnies exploded into a frenzy and came at me like a pack of zombies straight out of an old movie.

Eiggam sat back against a hut, arms crossed, and glared at me sanctimoniously.

"Stop, just stop!" Gunther cried. He thrust me off the circus grounds. "Stop, everybody, just step back and settle down! You!" Gunther roared as he stormed up to the enormous, glib god leaning casually observing the crowd. "Quit this. You and Maggie, stop this *right* now."

"Yeah. No." Eiggam shrugged.

I could see Gunther confronting the mighty being from my place in the buffer zone between our realms, but every time I tried to step forward to help him, the throng surged toward me hell-bent on my destruction. I didn't know if, at this point they could do it—honestly, I was losing track of every safeguard and means I had. We kept changing the rules.

Well, except for the capacity to kiss Gunther.

"This is ludicrous, huh?" Tabitha walked up beside me. I didn't respond, but she knew. I felt her hand reach out and brush my shoulder. "I feel like I'm caught in some weird HBO fantasy story where the writers were both drunk and perverse when they came up with this."

"How's Bob?" I asked her while continuing to watch Gunther and Eiggam. Their voices were too low for me to pick up, but they were debating something. Gunther's arms were flying and Eiggam's eyes rolling.

"Trying to change the subject?"

"Consideration for your boyfriend is changing the subject?"

"My...boyfriend," Tabitha said as if she was sampling the words for the first time and wasn't certain she'd like them. "You know, if he wasn't thousands of years old and non-human, I'd probably marry him. There's not a deceitful bone in the guy's body. Well, if he *has* bones. Do lares have bones?"

"I'd guess so. I never really thought about it."

"Yeah, I get it. Hard to run around wondering about all these strange beings all the time, I guess," Tabitha murmured and glanced back at the Magical Midway. "Yikes. Whatever that anger thing is? Devana's *all* kinds of crazy right now."

"Wait, what?" I craned my neck. "Devana and Ms. Elkins were fine, weren't they?"

Turning, I saw the ordinarily conservative Devana dressed like a porno princess warrior. She'd tied bones into her hair, and splashed herself sloppily with red paint—at least, I hoped it was red paint—across her face, arms, and torso like a warning.

A leather bikini barely concealed what it needed to cover. The staff-wielding huntress temporarily distracted every man—and not a few women.

"Devana?" I asked as I walked over to the Magical Midway. I almost stepped onto the fairgrounds but hesitated, my foot held high in the air. Slowly, I put it back down and shouted from outside the protections. "Are you all right?"

"You must *free* me from this confinement," she

howled like an animal. "Provide me passage from here. Now!"

"Um, so…it's like this. You look like a maniac," I explained to her. I leaned back away from the boundary just in case her staff had the reach her arms did not. "And you *sound* a little ragey, too. So, why don't you tell me what you would do if I let you out of here dressed like that?"

"Let me go!" she roared and thrust her staff at me forcefully. I dove out of the way, but not fast enough. The trenchant knife at the tip sank into my arm, and I yelped.

"For witches' sake, Devana, have you *lost your mind*?" I hollered. I buckled toward the ground, pain blinding my vision. It had been so long since I'd felt actual, honest-to-goodness physical discomfort that the intensity knocked me off my feet. "What the hell did you do that for?"

Devana's rage diminished, and her face turned white as she stood up. "You have no more armor?"

Tabitha kneeled beside me and scrutinized me. Concentrating, she grasped the staff in her hand reluctantly and I shrieked out again in pain. "I don't want to pull that out, I don't know enough about arms and blood and stuff to know whether it should stay in or come out. We have to get you to a hospital—"

"I am a healer, let me—"

"Don't you think maybe you've done enough?" Tabitha snapped at Devana. My human friend gave the huntress witch a glare so venomous that it rivaled Devana's mother. "Besides, I can't let you out, and I'm sure not passing *her* in to where *you* are. You people are all nuts right now."

"I am not, I can—"

"You can shut up," Tabitha told her. Turning back to me, she looked at me critically while Devana paced behind her like a caged cat. "How bad does it hurt?"

"Bad," I confessed through clenched teeth. I exhaled, trying to breathe through the pain, but all it did was make me dizzy. "It's been a couple of years since I've so much as stubbed a toe."

"I need to get Gunther," Tabitha said as she looked toward the Makepeace Circus.

I settled back on the ground, panted, and didn't argue as waves of nausea washed over me.

"Oh, no. No, no, no," Gunther said as I felt arms lift me from the ground. "How did this happen?"

"It's just an arm," I moaned.

"Devana wanted out, and she threw a staff with a knife on the end of it at her," Tabitha told him. I kept my eyes closed. "It looked ancient."

"Devana stabbed Charlotte with a *huntress glaive*?" Gunther asked her. I bounced in his arms. It felt like Gunther was running. My shoulder throbbed like someone was thrashing on it with a hammer as Gunther sputtered several saucy phrases that he typically would never have said. "Why would she *do* such a thing?"

"Who, the woman that murdered your father?" Tabitha asked sarcastically. "Gosh. No idea."

"Don't blame her," I stammered and swatted the air with my good arm. "She didn't—"

"Charlotte, my love, stop talking." Gunther gave me a tender squeeze. "I just want to get you to your parents' house and away from those cursed circuses before I heal you. You just rest. I've got you."

"You know, we're far enough away that a rock thrown couldn't reach," Tabitha said from someplace.

"I'm not sticking my wife on the ground in the dirt," Gunther snapped. I heard his feet thump against the stairs. "Besides, we're used to running from things. We always make sure we have a good distance if we can."

"That's not much of a life, Gunther," Tabitha responded softly. Gunther didn't respond.

"What *happened* to her?" my mother shouted and I smelled the familiar scents of her kitchen. "In there. Oh, dear me, look at all that blood. Alan? Alan! Come down here, Charlotte's been hurt!"

For the second time in my life, I was laid on the couch in my parents' house, damaged.

It was not lost on me that both times it took place, I was a ringmaster.

"I think she's coming around," my mother murmured. I felt cool moisture on my face. A cloth. My mother's soft washcloth. Her delicate hand swept a strand of hair from my cheek. "There's my girl. My poor girl. How do you feel, sweetheart?"

"Like I ate a rice ball before they cooked the rice," I whispered hoarsely. I lifted my injured arm, and even though it seemed tight, it didn't feel stabbed anymore. "I feel like I just went through surgery."

"You kind of did, so I imagine you feel all-around dreadful," my mother explained as my eyes focused on her concerned face. Pulling away the cloth, she exhaled and angled back toward the kitchen. "Give it a few minutes; you should feel better as your body reorients itself."

"Didn't Gunther just snap his fingers?" I asked as I battled to push myself up.

"Nope." Tabitha scrambled over to help me raise myself on the couch. "He was worried about all the craziness going on with the ringmaster powers, so he did it the old-fashioned way."

"Stitches?" I asked, startled, as I reached to feel the sewn-up wound.

"No, regular witch magic." My mother returned with a hot cup of tea and held it out to me. "Drink this; it should clear your head."

I took it and sipped. "Speaking of, where is Gunther?"

Tabitha and my mother glanced at one another, their expressions loaded with significance that I, in my impaired state, couldn't interpret. I waited, but neither one of them responded.

"Come on, spill. Where is he?" I demanded again after enough time had passed that I could safely assume neither one of them would tell me where he was, *and* that something was up.

There was an abrupt, terrible sound that shook the house on its foundations, and an orange glow briefly lit up the back window. As the trembling subsided, the dogs in the kennel howled and yelped.

"Oh, my," my mother murmured. She reached out to straighten a picture on the wall.

"What *was* that?" I asked.

"Your husband, I think," Tabitha said with a distinct lack of concern.

I struggled to my feet and headed for the back door, my mother and Tabitha urging me to slow down.

But neither of them would tell me what Gunther had gone to do, and I didn't know if that sound meant he succeeded, or he failed.

I was numb.

Bursting through the screen door, I felt like I should feel terror. Or panic. Worry. Fear. But I didn't.

I felt numb.

I dropped to my knees and gawked.

"So, what do you think?" Gunther, alive, asked gleefully.

My hands clutched each other so rigidly that my knuckles turned white as I stared at the pulsing blue radiant cube. Awestruck silence enveloped me. My staring eyes were accompanied by what I presumed was every citizen of both circuses—and yet I didn't think we, even jointly, could interpret what we were seeing. It was too shocking.

"Gunther, what did you do?" I whispered.

"Well, that's not the response I was hoping to get," Gunther said in a voice heavy with regret. "Come on, look past your shock. A neat solution, don't you think?"

"But...but how?" I choked out, still disbelieving.

"The same way they contained us," Gunther shrugged casually.

"Did you *imprison them*, son?" Roland Makepeace asked. He strode up with his wife, Gerda, and daughter, Anna.

"Impressive, huh, Dad?" Gunther asked.

"Why is your wife on her knees in the dirt?" Roland asked. Gunther jumped to help me up. "Did you try to get her in there, too, and it didn't work?"

"Dad!"

"Roland!"

"Oh, you two, calm down," Roland laughed at Gunther and Gerda. I glowered at my father-in-law, and he shrugged back at me. "You will really need to learn to take a joke, Charlotte. Especially if you're going to continue to be my daughter-in-law."

"What is going on out—Holy Frigg, what have you done, Makepeace?" Ms. Elkins gasped as she stared at the blue cube containing Gunther's hostages. "How could you do this?"

"Don't know. Just did," Gunther smiled and shrugged.

"What did you do, specifically?" Elkins marched up to him and shook a finger in his face.

"I just took the things we were using to divide the circus and combined it all up to contain them. And their energy," Gunther said to the old woman.

"*Why* would you do such a thing?" she choked. "How could you not check with me first?"

"Now, hold on there, norn," said Roland. "We ringmasters have been doing just fine without you for years—"

"Is that why all but *two* of you are helpless or dead?" she challenged him, jabbing a finger into his chest. Since he was incorporeal, it didn't have nearly the impact she intended it to. "Including *you*, dead guy? Your idiot son can't do this—"

"But I did," Gunther said, cutting her off.

"Oh, put a sock in it." Someone spoke from near my feet. "All of you."

"Who said that?" Roland demanded.

"It sounded like—" I said as I peered down. Two dark eyes peered up at me. "Samson?"

He yawned and angled his head.

"I heard him," Gunther said, staring down. "And not in my head."

"So did I," Roland added.

"Well, since you morons changed the rules of the game, the game is different," another voice from someplace around our feet claimed. "You know, when I agreed to be your familiar, blondie? This is not where I expected we would end up."

"Delilah?" Gunther gasped. The cat launched itself at him and scurried up his trunk to his shoulder. He grimaced. "Careful, claws."

"*Careful, claws,*" Delilah mimicked. "If you'd left your protection on, you boob, you wouldn't *have* that issue, would you?"

"What the *inferno* is going on here?" Roland demanded. "Why are the cats suddenly talking?"

"You imprisoned *stability* and *creativity* and

took their authority and power for yourselves. *Unrestrained* power, I might add," Samson drolled as he thrust his face toward Gunther. "They were controls on your power in the same way *you* were checks on theirs."

"Look at your rings, you morons," Delilah scoffed.

Gunther and I looked down at the lawgiver rings.

I knew before my eyes hit the gold circlet that it would be black, but it was unsettling to see it just the same.

CHAPTER 7

"I DON'T WANT ANYONE IN HERE," I SAID, PACING back and forth in my bedroom, to whoever had just opened the door.

"Tough," Tabitha slid inside the door and closed it securely behind her.

I turned and faced Tabitha. There was a piercing sense of apprehension, of worry, in her as she studied me. Yet her cool attitude, a nonchalant affectation she spent a childhood developing in response to her parents' constant quarrels, could make Tabitha seem cold, and remote. But I knew she wasn't.

She was fierce. When she needed to be.

"I sort of understand what the rings are, right?" my friend spoke as she moved toward my makeup counter and dragged out the chair. "You and Gunther are lawgivers, and those rings gave you powers or something, right?" I nodded. "And now, because they're black, they've passed some kind of judgment on you?"

"We're unredeemable," I explained to her. Okay, maybe not explained, really. Because I didn't have an explanation for how a ring just up and decided someone was a bad person and then turned itself off. "They no longer work."

"Yeah, but what does that *mean*, exactly? And how does a ring know who you are as a person?"

"I don't know, it just thinks we're evil? Horrible? Maybe there's a tiny little brain in it? I don't know how it works, Tabitha. Like all else in this world, it just is."

"*You* didn't lock the two gods into the big blue box," Tabitha pointed out. "So why would *your* ring turn black?"

"I don't *know*," I said again. "You're asking me a bunch of stuff I just don't know. I can't tell you."

"Well, *I* can tell *you* I wouldn't wear a magic ring on my finger without knowing what it was, what it could do, and what it meant," Tabitha said, looking over at me. "And the Charlotte Astley I knew in college never would have, either."

"I'm not that person anymore," I told her. I

pulled the black ring off my finger and dropped it with a clink on my bedside table.

Wait. What?

I turned and stared at in surprise, then my eyes narrowed. I didn't really think through taking it off, but I shouldn't have been able to take the ring from my finger. Aidan had told me that when it turned black it would fall off—the following morning when the sun rose.

Where the heck was Aidan, anyway?

"That was kind of my point," Tabitha broke into my thoughts and I looked up. "I just can't believe that we're all freaking out and obsessing over the color of two rings when all of those cats have disappeared, and your...Gunther jailed two gods on your back forty."

I spun away from her, but it didn't hinder the lecture she was working up to.

"Look, I'm not trying to line up behind the ring and pass judgment on any of you. It keeps being made clear to me in large and small ways that this, all this," Tabitha waved her arms in a sweeping gesture. "This isn't my world."

"It sounds like you are. Passing judgment, I mean," I told her distractedly, still studying the ring.

"I know it does, but...Look, Charlotte, you

just don't seem to have found your place yet," Tabitha said, and I firmly shook my head no, as Fiona and Anya walked in without knocking. "Now, before you get all defensive, just wait a second. Listen to me—"

"This doesn't have anything to do with you," Anya told Tabitha coldly, having only heard half of her statement. I sighed, sensing the dispute that was about to transpire. "This is paranormal business, human.

"Anya, don't." Fiona held up her hand. "The human is an acquaintance of Charlotte's. I don't like her, either, but she *is* the ringmaster's guest here."

Wow, I guess everyone was just expressing themselves today without a filter.

"Is she *even* a ringmaster anymore?" Anya yelled, her tone rising three octaves. She spun on her heel and jabbed her finger at Tabitha. "This is *your* error, human, we were all fine until our ringmaster abandoned us to race after you in some cave somewhere—"

Tabitha looked back calmly at the enraged nymph, her face stoic.

I sighed. "Don't talk to her like that, Anya, nothing is Tabitha's fault—"

"She's made you forget who you are!" Anya

shot back at my attempt to derail the throwdown that was about to occur in my bedroom. "Her, Gunther, being in this town! We have been here too long, we have been too wrapped up in human issues! You have forgotten your nature! And *that human*," Anya spat with all the derision she could infuse into two words. "That human, most of all, is responsible for it!"

"No, she isn't," I sighed, my eyes swelling with tears as I sat down with a thump on the bed. "She hasn't made me forget. If anything, she's been trying to remind me who I was...before all this. That I was someone before I was this. Before magic rings, before Council attacks, before gods and powers and alternative realities and—"

"Before *us*, you mean?" Fiona asked dispassionately. "Before us, before Gunther. Back when we were just a holiday you took once a year, a pen pal, a fuzzy voice at the other side of a cauldron call—"

"That's not what I meant. That's not fair—" I tried to argue, but Anya cut me off.

"None of this is *fair*, Charlotte," Anya deadpanned.

"Look, this is my life—"

"No. It is *all* of our lives," Fiona said sharply.

She crossed her arms and stared down at me. "Do you still not understand that? Even now?"

"You don't think that's a lot of pressure to put on one person?" Tabitha asked from her seat.

"Human, I'm warning you," Fiona spoke in a low, shaky voice, her uncommonly angry eyes glued to Tabitha's serene, amused ones. Tabitha chuckled and shook her head. Turning back to me, Fiona held out her hand. "Anya may be saying things less than respectfully, but her challenge *is* appropriate. *Are* you even a ringmaster anymore?"

I stared at Fiona, startled at the suggestion. "What does *that* mean? Of course I am!"

"Your husband has robbed us of our dome to enclose the two spirits in the cube," Fiona said. "Dergal reports that the centaur village is slowly decreasing as our energy is siphoned off to contain them. *What* is the plan?"

"I don't know," I told her hotly. "I didn't *do* it! Ask Gunther!"

"And this is why I say you are *no* ringmaster!" Anya scoffed. "You have given your power to a man! You keep the counsel of a human! You—"

"Oh, for the love of Pete, just *get out*," I told Anya wearily and sank my head in my hands. I heard Fiona and Anya arguing with one another about the best way to get through to me (with Anya leaning toward torture and Fiona advocating for talk).

Suddenly, I heard Anya storm out with a string of angry curses. Peering up after the door slammed, I found Fiona staring at me quietly as she paused next to Tabitha.

"I'm going, Charlotte, so no need for you to renew your desire for me to leave you *alone*. Before I leave, I want to remind you of one thing," Fiona said.

I waited.

After several moments, in a voice so deathly quiet it made my stomach seize up, she said, "You chose this. And all that flowed from that judgment can be traced back to that choice, that one choice, you made to become ringmaster of this circus."

"I know that," I told her. Fiona's expression clearly indicated she did not believe me. Not at all. But she didn't say it.

"Perhaps," Fiona agreed gently. "But when you chose, you chose for all of us. We got no vote. We had no say. Your next choice? You will again be determining the future for all of us. If you must do that alone, I understand," she said, glancing at Tabitha. "But choose carefully, Charlotte."

Fiona glanced at Tabitha, turned, and slipped out the door.

Tabitha and I sat silently in my bedroom as I ran through everything that had happened, everything that everyone had said to me.

Everyone was right…

…and everyone was wrong.

"Oh, for God's sake," I muttered to myself, thoroughly overwhelmed. "How is one person supposed to think through all this?"

The Galenite cats were missing.

Eiggam and Maggie were trapped in a big blue box.

The citizens of the circuses were no longer crazed berserkers, thanks to Gunther's confinement of the two angry gods, but now the citizens were unprotected—and I didn't even know if that mattered. Did the Witches' Council have any means of attack anymore?

Mina *could* just throw a punch, I snorted. My nose could be broken now. Arm broken. I could be stabbed. Felled by a sword. Trip over a misplaced bucket.

And then it hit me.

Everything was about power.

The power to influence, to protect, to attack. Everything that had happened to us could be tracked back to that single motivation. The quest for power. Who had it, who wanted it, who wanted to take it from somewhere else so they could have more of it.

The Witches' Council wanted power over us.

Maggie and Eiggam wanted power over each other.

The citizens of the circuses wanted someone more powerful than them to protect them.

It was, quite ironically, so very human if you thought about it long enough.

"What are you thinking about?" Tabitha asked.

"How Gunther and I, through various blunders and acts that meant well, have kind of upended the whole power structure of the paranormal world," I told her as I looked up. "I mean, take what's just happened in the past two days. All we wanted to do was be able to kiss, and now he and I can be wiped out and two gods are in jail."

"There's always a price," Tabitha reminded me in a matter-of-fact tone.

"Yeah, well, at this point my bank account's ability to keep paying is starting to dwindle down to nothing," I said. "I'm spent. It's enough already."

"So change it," Tabitha nodded.

"What do you mean *change it?*"

"She means just what she said, Charlotte," Samson said from high above me. I strained my neck and glanced up to see the black cat leisurely splayed across my top bookshelf. "Change it."

"How long have *you* been there?"

"Long enough to attend the fight as well as the subsequent pity party afterward," he said, and then he yawned. His tail swished as he looked down at me in that judgmental way he had.

"Why can everyone hear you now?" I called up. "Well, you and Delilah. Where is she, by the way?"

"Attending Gunther's pity party, no doubt." Samson stretched upwards and began zig-zagging down the shelves. "Tabitha is right. You and he have the power to change things right now. And the norn won't inform you of it."

"Why not?"

"Because she's ancient, and she doesn't want things to change. At least not more than she has helped to change." Samson dropped to the floor and promptly hopped up onto my bed. He butted his head against my hand and I lifted it tentatively. "You *know* where my ear is. Scratch it. Many things may have just changed, but that *certainly* has not."

Tabitha chuckled.

I scratched it, and as I scratched, there was a knock at the door.

"Charlotte? It's Mercy. Can I come in?"

Great. Just what I needed. A member of the Witches' Council walking into all this. Because clearly, I didn't have enough to figure out.

"Take it," Mercy said, holding out a dusty old scroll to me.

I stared at it and assessed it, though what I was looking for, I couldn't really tell you. A red glow? A sign wrapped around it that said *Read Me*? It was just a scroll, like any other scroll I'd ever seen.

I mean, not that I'd seen many.

"Yeah, not without you telling me why," I said, holding my palms up.

"Take it," Samson said.

"Same thing," I said, turning to look at the cat.

Samson sneezed.

"It is the magic that holds the paranormal

world apart from the human one," Mercy explained as she held it out. "Well, not the scroll itself. The spell that created the divide. I managed to take it while Mina was ranting and raving about the renunciation of Eiggam. Within this scroll—"

"You can bring the worlds together," Samson finished.

I gritted my teeth and squinted at the scroll Mercy held out. Of course I was just finding out about its existence now. Of course no one had bothered to tell me such a thing existed before now.

"It is the spell that powers the mists," Mercy finished, continuing to hold the scroll toward me.

I had no idea what the mists were. "And why are you giving it to me? Why now?"

"Eiggam had cast protections around it so that no one could lay their hands on it," she told me. "It took a great power to pull our worlds apart, to separate the paranormal towns from the world and make it impossible for humans to wander into our realms. As your circuses managed to breach that divide, perhaps you can undo it."

"Why would I want to do that?"

"Paranormals have become *more* paranormal over the years, more and more distant from the world." Samson hopped up on my desk, his tail straight up in the air. With a flick, he added, "They're kind of like cats in that way."

"That still doesn't explain why I'm—"

"You were told you would have to make a choice," Mercy said respectfully. Her composure was coldly patient, but I could see that was wearing thin as her eyes pinched. "This is the choice. This is the apex of the prophecy. We were of the world. We can be again. You *have* to take it."

"Just take it," a squeaky voice said from somewhere near the rafters. I craned my neck and scanned the wooden rafters at the top of the yurt and spotted the little death bat, Cama, in the corner. "Mercy is going to hold it out to you and keep squawking until you take it. She has to."

"What do you mean? Why does she *have* to?" I called up.

"Because *my* mother helped her get it and bring it to you," Cama said with a flap. "And if you don't take it like Mom wants, she's going to show up here and *make* you take it."

The mere mention of the frightening woman that was mother to that bat seized my innards. We had met Cama's "mother" here in Mickwac when she came to take the souls of two not-so-nice people to their ever-after suffering.

To say they didn't look happy to go with her was an understatement.

To say she was blood-curdlingly menacing would, also, be an understatement.

"Give me the damn scroll," I said, snatching it from Mercy's hand.

CHAPTER 8

TABITHA AND I SCANNED THE WORDS IN THE scroll and Mercy stood back, observing us. "I don't understand," I mumbled when I reached the bottom. "I thought *we* hid the paranormal world from the human world for the safety of the paranormals?"

"I presume there are many things that you have been told that are distorted," Mercy shrugged indifferently.

"So, if this thing is to be believed, it was *humans* that hid the paranormal world, and *not* the other way around," Tabitha said as she leaned up and looked at me. "Are you *sure* that someone said the paranormals hid *themselves*?"

"Yeah, I mean, that's what they teach, I think."

Tabitha looked at Mercy. "How does Charlotte know that this scroll is telling the truth?"

"It is," Cama squeaked. "Mom said."

"And how do we know your mother—" Tabitha started, but I cut her off.

"Don't. Don't speak ill of Cama's mother. Just trust me on this one. We don't want her showing up here to defend her point of view."

"Does it matter?" Mercy asked Tabitha. "The truth or lie of the origin of the divide is unimportant, isn't it? Does it really matter how it happened?"

"Well, I feel like it should matter," Tabitha responded sounding unsure. "Truth of history is important, right?"

"What matters is they *forced it*," Mercy said, answering her own question. "The two worlds were not *intended* to be separated. Paranormals were not intended to live in fairyland becoming more and more subjected to magic, and the humans were not intended to live without magic."

"Says you," I pointed out.

"Says me," Mercy agreed. "You can fix it."

"Look, there's a lot of other stuff going on and I think we could handle this after we deal with the Galenite cats and Maggie and Eiggam out there in the glowing jail—"

"You are incorrect," Mercy told me. "The only reason you have a chance to correct this perversion is because the two angels that broke the world are locked in that box."

"Wait a minute. They did this?" I asked her, astonished. I looked down at the scroll and scoured for any mention of any names that would indicate Maggie and Eiggam had carried out this...well, imprisoning of the paranormals and their own small region of the world.

"Did you read about the two angels?" Mercy asked, rolling her eyes. "The capricious beings that determined the two worlds must be eternally divided after the humans prevailed upon them to do so?"

"Yes," I nodded. "But—"

"Did the nature of their arrogance *remind* you of anyone?" the witch asked, her eyes moving from the scroll to me. One eyebrow raised.

"Oh, come on. They can't be the *only* two haughty, obnoxious beings in the entire universe."

"I suspect not, but they *are* the only two that seemed to be infatuated with breaking things," Mercy pointed out. "Not that I know all pompous, obnoxious beings in the entire universe, but I was on the Witches' Council. I do know many. Most are not especially concerned with the human or paranormal worlds."

"But these two are."

Mercy nodded.

"If this is true," I pointed to the scroll, "that means everything that's happened since paranormals have been hidden has been nothing more than two beings with too much power making unilateral decisions for the world, because they can."

"Well, it's not just because they *can*," Tabitha pointed out. "It's because they think they know better. It's a power-over situation."

"*Do* they know better?" I murmured to myself.

"You have dealt with them," Mercy replied, her arms crossed again. "What do *you* think?"

"I think they're capricious idiots. But they're powerful capricious idiots. They are crazy and they are foolhardy and they are powerful."

"Not at the moment, they're not," Samson said.

I left my yurt alone and walked out onto the Magical Midway, while Mercy and Tabitha worked together to condense the scroll down into the points we needed to get across to the others. While heading toward the Makepeace Circus, I reached out with my ringmaster power to take stock of how the citizens were feeling.

With a start I discovered it—my power, my connection to everyone—had faded.

I couldn't seek out people and recognize precisely where they were. I couldn't feel the thoughts and feelings of the entire collective the way I could before. I was supposedly even more powerful than I had *ever* been—and yet much of what had made me linked to this place and these people seemed like a transmission just out of sync.

The Magical Midway as it had been was already changing, and I didn't need telepathy to recognize that people were afraid.

"Charlotte," Samantha Goodfellow called from within Fortuna's fortune-telling tent. I halted and shifted around, stepping over to the priestess. "You look like you've seen a phantom," she told me pleasantly.

"Just thinking, Ms. Goodfellow," I explained to her as I entered the candlelit enclosure. "Are you all doing all right? I know things have become a little crazy tonight."

"This is all *incredibly* interesting," she replied with a giddy elation, and slapped me hard on the back. I winced. She was stronger than she looked. "What an astonishing evening, my dear!"

"Well, I'm overjoyed that we could entertain you," I responded. As I turned to leave, Fortuna's hand reached out to stop me.

"Charlotte, I would like to give you a reading," she informed me with that intensity she had.

"A reading? Like a sit down and get my fortune told thing?"

Fortuna nodded.

For the most part, I always understood that Fortuna simply read people's minds as the norm of how she operated. So, her question sounded odd, and I *didn't* really grasp what she was talking about.

Regardless, I had other things to do.

"I don't really have time, Fortuna. You can read my mind, so you know everything I'm dealing with—"

"I cannot, actually," Fortuna told me, blushing. My face must've expressed unease, because she quickly waved at me. "No, no, it's not that I *can't* read your mind. I've been chatting quite extensively with the priestess about the moralities that the human witches agree to keep."

"Oh?"

"They have a very rigid understanding of consent, something that we…don't seem to have," Fortuna explained as Samantha Goodfellow nodded behind her. "They don't read people without their permission. I found priestess Goodfellow's explanation for that self-control very logical, actually."

"Are you a member of the coven now?" I asked, laughing.

But my laugh faded when Fortuna did not laugh in response.

"I am not," Fortuna smiled. "It takes much longer than a few weeks to do that. Priestess Goodfellow has given me a lot to think about, though, about what it means to be a witch and how my powers can violate other people without my meaning to. You know, the right and wrong of what I do—especially when someone doesn't know what I can do."

"It's also difficult to have an honest communication with *anyone* when you can read their minds," Sarah Stevens added, nodding earnestly. "It's lopsided. Completely. It's a situation *rife* with the potential for misuse and grief. Better for *everyone* that there's consent."

"Priestess Goodfellow also instructed me on

the use of tarot cards and crystal balls." Fortuna pointed to the tools I always presumed to be only affectation. "It acts as a focus, and a self-imposed limitation on my power, in some ways."

I listened to the telepath, and then I noticed she looked…*different*. Her face was more relaxed, and she was smiling more. And her hair—

"Holy highlights, Fortuna, *what* did you do your *hair*?" I asked, squinting. In the dark, the thick blonde highlights she had added to her chestnut brown locks seemed to glow. "Did you *tint* your hair?"

"We're getting off track," Fortuna said, astonishing me yet again. She had always been a quiet woman, serious, a little unsettled by her place in the world. She was also invariably a little…well, *intimidated* by me. If you want to know the truth, I had grown used to it.

She also never used a *contraction* before, her voice always crisp and defined, the proper rich girl boarding school accent clear. Or maybe it was just its use coupled with all the other changes that made me notice it more.

Whatever emotional or metaphysical work she had been doing with the witches of Avalon Grove, it had *clearly* produced an effect.

"Sorry," I apologized. "I really don't have time for a reading, though—"

"*I* think perhaps you should." Samantha Goodfellow planted her two feet astride the entrance. The ample girth wrapped around the chubby priestess's frame blocked my exit, and she held her hand out toward the chair.

Like I said, apparently everybody was running without a filter today.

I nodded, and Fortuna and I moved to her reading table.

~

I left Fortuna's yurt shaken.

She informed me of a few things, none that appeared to have been pulled directly out of my head. All seemed prophetic, information that was beyond mere telepathy.

One was that she believed Gunther was my soul mate—honestly, that wasn't *all* that shocking. It was nice to have it confirmed—even if I didn't wholly trust what she was telling me.

At least not then.

The second was that I would be the ringmaster that destroyed the last of the circuses. Fortuna divulged this to me as if she was in a trance—and she refused, even when I pressed her, to say whether this was a good or bad thing. She told me nothing about how it would come to pass.

The third was that Mina World was coming.

"Have you seen Gunther?" I asked Bob as I trudged toward the Makepeace Circus again.

"Not since he put our benefactors in the Big Blue Box, no ma'am," Bob informed me coldly over his shoulder, racing past me. "If you'll *excuse* me, Charlotte, since the Magical Midway's bounds are gone my patrol area's gotten a *little* cumbersome."

"What do you mean?" I called after him. The lares stopped, and his shoulders slumped. It was a little disconcerting seeing the happy hippie lares so discombobulated.

"I'm a household protector," Bob snapped. He twisted on his heel and marched back to me. "Your husband just made the household *way bigger* than I'm used to, and we're not integrating with the gargoyles so…" He threw up his hands in irritation. "Doing the best I can under the circumstances. *Ma'am.*"

"Well, I'm sorry you have to *walk* a little more," I told him with a little tinge of sarcasm. His eyes narrowed. "And I loathe to make your evening *even* worse, but Fortuna just told me something that you guys probably should know," I said. And then I related what Fortuna had told me about Mina World.

"Oh, that's just *great!*" Bob yelled with fury. He threw his spear down on the ground. "Like we don't have *enough* going on! Anything *else* you want to do? Declare war on the humans, maybe? Put the lions in a cage with the tigers and have them fight it out? Great! Just *great!*" he shouted as he paced.

I stared at Bob.

"My mother is coming *here?*" Devana, warrior berserker, said as she stepped up to the two of us. The paint on her face had been smeared, but she still looked as savage as ever.

"Are you going to *stab* her again?" Bob asked her in anguish. He leaned over and jerked up his spear. "Because if you're gonna try to stab her again, I'm gonna *have* to attack you and protect *her*, and honestly I'm kind of *annoyed* with her. I *absolutely* don't want to."

"Geez, Bob, thanks a lot," I told him.

"You have really, seriously, fully *killed my Zen*! I worked *really hard* for that Zen, and suddenly in *one night* you and your husband just stomped all over it! *All over it!*" Bob yelled at me. "*All over my Zen!*"

"Are *you* going to whack her?" Devana asked Bob uneasily.

"I wish I could!" he roared. He hopped up and down, and I jumped back, just in case. "But I'm a lares! We can't stab the individuals we're expected to protect! *Not even if they deserve it!*"

I didn't know what to say, so I stayed mum while the lares panted.

The silence was long.

And uncomfortable.

Finally, Bob spoke again, his finger pointed in my face. "Never let it be said the Larry brothers didn't do their job, even when our boss is a Zen killer. *Zen killer!*" he cried at me one more time. Then he whirled on his heel and left.

"That is a *very* peculiar man," Devana said. We watched him stomp off. The huntress witch turned to me and her eyes softened as they flashed toward my shoulder. "Charlotte, I am mortified that I—"

"Devana, you *didn't* know. I don't blame you. Gunther healed me, and everything turned out fine."

"We can cripple or kill you with a human

weapon," Devana said with grave concern. "I would hardly call that *fine*, Charlotte."

"What's this?" Aidan said as he strolled up with Kyle.

"You have no idea, no idea at all, what's been going on here?" I asked him. As I began speaking, his eyes sparkled and his face darkened. By the middle of the sentence, he grimaced. By the time I reached the end of the question, he was horrified.

"*Now* I do," Aidan choked out as his past reader power absorbed from me in the span of that one sentence all he had missed. "For goodness sake, Charlotte, we were *only* in town for two days!"

"What is that big blue box?" Kyle asked.

As Aidan, Devana and I described to Kyle what had ensued while the two of them were visiting acquaintances in town the past two days, the centaur's horrified expression eventually mirrored his boyfriend's.

CHAPTER 9

As I scaled the steps to Gunther's cabin, I heard shouts so crude they would've caused a trucker to blush. "And another thing!" Wayland Black yelled as I gradually pushed wide the front door. Gunther was perched on the couch, his head in his hands. "If you're all mighty and *whatever* now, why don't you just resurrect yer pappy so we can get some real leadership again before we're *all* dead!"

"Am I disturbing?" I inquired brightly. Gunther's head raised from his hands and his mouth opened to speak, but Wayland Black cut him off.

"*You*," the cyclops growled savagely, his one huge eye narrowed. "This is all your responsibility. Everything was fine before you showed up, and then you screwed this boy around your cute little finger. His father up and croaks, all the cats disappear...Is there anything you see that you don't wreck, girl?"

"Is *this* how you all deal with an emergency over at the Makepeace Circus?" I challenged him. "Because if it *is*, I *think* I can spot your issue. And it isn't me."

With a bark, Wayland Black lunged at me, his massive, callused hands thrust out as he made for my throat. Gunther shot to his feet and shoved himself in between the raging cyclops and me.

"Gunther, be careful!" I shrieked.

With a howl of rage, the two men collided.

And the two men were not equally matched.

Wayland Black seemed to get control of himself precisely a second too late, and he lurched backward. Gunther was moving backward as well, but the momentum was from the force of the collision. I watched in dread as the gentlest man I knew flew through the air toward the wall.

"Stop!" I shouted instinctively moving toward him.

Gunther's body stopped midair, seven feet off

the ground, and lingered there as if halted by a giant hand.

"Thanks," he panted and jerked himself upright. He spun as if suspended, able to move his body and pivot around like his belly button had bound him to that spot. No matter how much he jerked, twirled, and struggled he could not reach the floor.

I tried not to snicker.

"I, um...can you let me down, maybe?" Gunther stared at me hopefully as he came to a slow halt upside down.

"Go down!" I cried, and he shot to the floor.

"Ow!" Gunther jerked his hand up and rubbed it. "I'm really not used to that. The whole pain thing. That takes some getting used to all over again."

"You okay?"

"It could have been worse," Gunther nodded.

"Holy Uranus, the two of you are *utter idiots.*" tThe blacksmith gawked at us incredulously. "Generations of ringmasters, and *this* is what we wound up with? I'm glad my father isn't alive to see this. It would disgrace him."

"Oh, calm down," I told him and helped Gunther off the floor. He stumbled back toward the couch. "No one's dead—"

"Yet."

"Have you tried to find out anything about the Galenite cats disappearing, or have you just wasted your time yelling at Gunther because they're gone?" I asked, casting a skeptical glimpse at Wayland.

"I don't answer to you," Wayland Black insisted.

"I just asked a question. You can't just answer a question?"

"I'm too busy to snap to every time you look for clarity on something you should have clarity on since you caused it," he countered indignantly.

I couldn't even follow that one. "So, why am *I* getting blamed for the cats?" I asked Gunther.

"Everything was *fine* until you showed up," Wayland answered for Gunther before he could even open his mouth to form the words. "This is all your fault! Everything that's happened to us, every catastrophe that we've had to deal with! You two are cursed! Cursed!"

"You know, I have to tell you, I'm not *really* in the frame of mind for any of this," I told Wayland shortly. I leaned up and turned toward him.

Taking a deep breath, I tried to calm myself.

"Look, Wayland, I *get* that lot of stuff has happened since Gunther and I met. I understand that everyone involved in the circuses may believe the fault lies in the other circus, with the other ringmaster—"

"It doesn't lie with the other circus, it lies with you! You and your circus!"

"Are you even listening to me?" I asked him, incredulous.

"No!" he shouted.

I glared at him and tried again.

"Look, the circuses were basically *redoubts*. You know what that is?" I asked him. Without waiting for him to respond, I continued. "Historically, they were fortified defensive encampments. Redoubt literally means *a place of retreat*. The thing about redoubts is that they're not *part* of anything. They were military fortifications *outside* of the main defensive line."

"What does this have to do with anything?" Wayland asked me.

"We, the circuses, were not fully part of the human world. We were not fully part of the paranormal world. We stayed *outside* of that, defensive to the human world that they might discover us. Defensive to the paranormal world that they might end us," I spelled out, clarity coming as I spoke. "We weren't a part of *anything*, Wayland. We hid. We defended ourselves."

"Well, yes, that's why—"

"We were a place to hide."

"Yes, yes, that's why—"

"Eventually, what you're hiding from? It *finds* you. It's found us, that's *all*," I clarified gently as the lone eye softened and blinked. "Gunther and I are, a bit, a part of everything, though. Human *and* paranormal."

Gunther gasped.

"It's why this is all going on now," I finished. "At least, I *think* it is."

"It's why the decision falls to us," Gunther whispered.

"No one can hide forever," I shrugged as Gunther rose to his feet.

Suddenly a cat howled from the corner of the room.

I looked up to see Samson, his fur puffed up and his head pulled back, glaring at Delilah. Her paw was raised forward as if she had just whacked him on the nose.

"Your human is not as dumb as I thought she was," Delilah told Samson. Gunther smiled at his familiar's commentary.

∾

Wayland Black sat in a corner drinking out of a liquor bottle. "But I *liked* things the way they were," he mumbled drunkenly to himself. The cats punctuated his drunken murmurings by with delicate, drowsy purrs.

"You really believe all that stuff you just told him?" Gunther asked me in a low voice. I explained to Gunther about the scroll, and Fortuna's reading. I added some of my other observations, like the fact that Ethel Elkins had not left her room since this all started.

"I don't know why she's not getting involved in all this when she's been so involved in everything else," I pointed out. "But Devana's dressed up like *Xena, Warrior Princess* and I haven't seen her with the norn in a good while.",

"What is a *Xena, Warrior Princess*?" Gunther asked me.

"When this is all over, you and I are gonna spend a lot of time catching up on a lot of cultural moments that you've missed from the human world," I grinned as Wayland continued to talk sharply to himself. My laugh trailed off, and I grew serious. "Have you found out anything about the Galenite cats?"

"There's no blood, nothing that looks like there was a battle," Gunther said as he leaned back against the couch. "It's like every one of them, the cursed witches and the regular cats, just vanished."

"Do you think they just left?" I asked and Gunther looked at me sharply.

"Why would you ask that?"

"Well, with the border down…I don't know, I mean, they didn't seem very talkative when they were here. So, if they just wandered off, would anyone even know?"

Gunther considered my point and then shrugged. "Surely they've heard about the Witches' Council curse to *do unto others*. Maybe they realized there was nothing to be afraid of anymore."

"Hey!" I smiled. "That's a human reference."

Gunther looked mildly offended. "I *listen* when you speak, you know." Then he winked. "In any case, they didn't tell Delilah that they were leaving. She hung out with them all the time."

I nodded, and we fell silent. Gunther reached across for my hand and grasped it. The feel of his skin, the warmth of him, was still a surprising thing to me. After a few moments, I said hesitantly, "Can I ask you something?"

"You can always ask me anything, Charlotte," he answered and squeezed my hand.

"Why aren't *you* freaking out?" Gunther's face assumed an expression of confusion. "What I mean is, it seems like *every* paranormal is losing their minds." I pointed to the back corner of the room where a gibbering, drunk Wayland Black was debating intently with the wall. "It also seems like the humans, or people from the human world, are not. Samantha Goodfellow seems excited. Fortuna doesn't seem bothered by anything. Tabitha is taking the whole thing in stride."

"Well, that stands to reason. It's not happening to *their* world."

"I don't know that I agree with that, but again, that's not my question. *You* are a paranormal, and you're not freaking out. *Why* are you not freaking out?"

"You mentioned before that Aidan and Kyle seemed a little anxious, so I don't know that the partition line is as exacting as you make it out to be," Gunther said as he looked back critically at Wayland Black and rolled his eyes. "But as to your question concerning why I am calm?"

I nodded. Gunther grew quiet, his hand still in mine. His head bowed, he gazed off thoughtfully. After a few moments, he spoke.

"My mother was killed when I was young. My

father was overcome by misery and anger and booze. I grew up an outcast, half witch, and the son of a ringmaster, one of the most feared witches in the paranormal world," he told me, his face flashing with remembered pain.

I nodded.

"Since I met you? My mother's been returned to me, and I have a new sister. My father's been made whole again, and he's happy. I don't know that I feel any different being a full witch, but I know it feels good to belong."

Gunther got up and kneeled down in front of me. Taking my hands in his, he grinned. "I'm not freaking out because despite what *everyone* thinks about the changes that are happening? From my viewpoint, your existence is a gift."

"But—"

"You *heal* things that are broken. My life has done nothing but improve since I met you, and I know whatever we suffer through? Things will be better in the end."

Gunther leaned forward and kissed me.

As we pulled away, Wayland Black belched.

CHAPTER 10

GUNTHER AND I LEFT THE INTOXICATED, DROOLING
Wayland to his spirited discussion with the wall.
As soon as our feet struck the bottom steps, a
crowd rushed toward us.

"What are the two of you going to do to fix
this?"

"Are the circuses shutting down?"

"Where would we go?"

"What are we to do?"

"Tell us, Ringmaster! Tell us what is going on!"

"You all step back from ringmaster now,"
Ambom said roughly, elbowing his way to the
front. A dingy-looking leprechaun glared at the
gargoyle driving the crowd forcefully away from
us. "Give ringmaster space. And probably lady

ringmaster, too, even though big blue cube all her fault."

"I didn't put Maggie and Eiggam in the cube!" I told him with irritation. "My *husband* did that. You know, *your* ringmaster?"

"Way to be supportive, honey," Gunther said, sounding a little injured.

"Well, you did! It's not *my* fault you did it."

"We think everything your fault," Ambom shrugged.

"The gargoyle may be dumb as a rock—"

"Hey! Just because I'm rock doesn't mean I'm dumb!"

"Yeah, yeah, sure," the gnome said with one eyebrow slightly raised. "Anyway, he's right. My expertise is luck, girl, and you're about as unlucky as they come." Gunther glared at the short man and took a deep breath.

"Folks, go back to your cabins, gather in the public house if you'd like, and let us do what we need to do to find the cats and deal with the issue—"

"That she created, you mean," the leprechaun glanced pointedly back over his shoulder at me.

"That's enough. I'll gather you all up when we have something to share," Gunther irritably waved the leprechaun toward the living areas.

As the crowd dissipated, I leaned over to Gunther and whispered, "Everyone's concern will only grow the longer we don't give them any information, you know. I doubt it's any better over at my place."

"I think you and I have to visit the big blue box."

I gawked at him incredulously. "Are you crazy? I'm not going in there!"

"Well, think about it," Gunther said. "Maybe locking them up was impetuous, and we're certainly seeing things that I didn't expect—like the barriers coming down. But they established the situation. They presumably have the answers —or, at least, more knowledge about what's going on than we have. I don't want to keep stumbling around guessing, do you?"

"We have no armor!"

"I don't know that our armor ever worked against them, anyway, so don't think we will really be in a different situation than we normally are—"

"We are in a hugely different position, Gunther—you stuck them in a box! And we are each an agent of one of them—what if they can manipulate us somehow the way Mina controlled you that time?" I asked him, shivering at the recollection.

"Do you have a better idea?" Gunther asked me sincerely.

The problem was, I really didn't.

"Let's solve the issue with the cats first?" I asked hopefully. "And then worry about the gods in the box?"

"We're just going to be stalling for time," Gunther smiled tenderly at me. "Maybe I'm developing intuition, but I just don't believe that they're in any danger. The cats, I mean. I assume I would feel it."

"I can't sense my circus the way I used to anymore, so I *wouldn't* hang your hat on that feeling," I told him.

"I don't wear a hat," Gunther said, confusion writ clear across his handsome face.

"It's a—oh, never mind, come on." I gripped his hand and yanked him toward my circus. "Let's check with Aidan first before we do anything. He supposedly knows everything that's ever happened, or something. Maybe he can give us some insight that will help us decide what to do next."

"Anything I can do to help, Charlotte," Aidan said. We sat in the familiar room back at my dorm yurt. "Keep in mind I have never been around Eiggam, only Maggie," Aidan reminded me. Though his talent gave him access to all aspects and threads of the past, he had to have direct contact with someone to access their string. "While I was around her only briefly, I understand her nature."

"*I've* been around them both," Cama, the death bat, squeaked from the rafters. "Aunt Maggie and Uncle Eiggam came to my two-thousand and seventy-first birthday party!"

The four of us—Aidan, Kyle, Gunther and I— turned to peer at the small bat in the corner. Her ringing peals of laughter echoed like a rapidly chittering bird punctuated by rough squawks.

"Okay, then what are they fighting over?" I quizzed her.

"Well, *you*, of course," Cama said matter-of-factly.

"Me?" I asked, confused.

"No, not you as in *just* you, silly," Cama said exasperatedly. She rushed down and settled in my hair.

Although the bat had been with us a few months and had executed no one, she *was* a death bat. My innards seized up with the recognition that the grim reaper had nested in my hair, and I no longer had any shield against her.

"Okay, who then?" I choked out, trying not to overreact.

"Like, all of you. Humans, paranormals, beasts, butterflies, amoebas…You know. Everyone. That's why everyone's showing up here."

"I'm sorry, everyone's *what* now?" I asked the bat.

The front door crashed open, and Roland Makepeace, his dark face furious, stalked across the room to the four of us. "Get the norn under control!" he howled. "She won't listen to me!"

"Dad, what's—"

"Roland Makepeace, you are the most intractable, absurd, dimwitted—" Ms. Elkins shouted as she shuffled in behind him. A worried looking Gerda Makepeace trailed the old woman. Little Anna hid behind her mother and peeped out at the adults with fear.

"She's part of your circus, daughter-in-law," Roland snorted. He crossed his arms and planted his feet in the ground. "Can you get that woman under some kind of control? Or throw her in the box with the others so I don't have to listen to her. Something!"

"*What's* going on?" I asked. He started pacing and she proceeded to shuffle casually toward the rocking chair. "Ms. Elkins, where have you been? And why is Gunther's dad so angry at—"

"Oh, Roland was always a cantankerous old goat," the norn waved her hand negligently as if brushing aside a troublesome fly. "He just missed being a complete son of a—"

"Ms. Elkins!' I shouted.

"Keep your knickers on, Charlotte," Ms. Elkins grumbled as she hurled herself down into the cushioned armchair. "Old grumpy over there just seems to think the fact that he's a dead ringmaster gives him some kind of say about what's going on, and he doesn't appreciate it when I tell him it *doesn't*."

"The woman is hopeless. Impossible!" Roland told his wife, Gerda, who sought to assuage his outburst.

"What is the controversy between the two of you?"

"There is no—" Ms. Elkins began.

"That woman wants to move the circuses to the ringmaster realm!" Roland said with indignation. "Forever!"

"Wait, you mean that place that we go when

the circus is passed from ringmaster to ringmaster?" I asked.

"Yes! Permanently! That woman wants to take these people, pick them up and imprison them in that place so they never connect with this world again! Have you ever heard of such ridiculous hogwash? Ridiculous. Ridiculous!"

"I would advise you not to get yourself so excited, Roland, but you're already dead," Ms. Elkins deadpanned. She dragged out her knitting. "Let me point out again for those in the back," she said, "you're deceased. The dead have no say."

"If *I* don't have a say, what makes you think you have a say?" Roland demanded.

"Because your son imprisoned the two beings that animate this place," she explained to him patiently. The old woman's eyes rose from her yarn and she frowned up at him from behind her glasses. "Or did you forget that in one night, your untrained, undisciplined offspring committed an act that dropped the perimeter and precipitated the last two lawgiver rings in existence to turn black?"

Gunther turned red with embarrassment and I reached out to squeeze his hand.

"You know, you lived at the Makepeace Circus longer than you lived here," Roland spat bitterly.

"Maybe if you had troubled to bring up your task in all this, he might not have been so untrained or undisciplined that—"

"Look, we've made mistakes before," I told her, cutting off Roland's rant. "He and I can fix—"

"Not like *this*, you haven't," Ms. Elkins said with uncharacteristic solemnity. "You have outraged the gods. You have played with forces you don't understand. There is only *one* barrier left now to protect these people. And it is in the ringmaster realm."

"Protect them from what?"

"She says if we don't get the circuses there, they will be forever eradicated," Roland told us.

"By who?" Gunther asked.

I heard the echo of Fortuna's reading in Roland's words, but I said nothing.

"Mama, are we going to have to leave here?" Anna whispered from behind Gerda's skirt. "Did Gunther do something bad?" Gerda hushed the slight girl ghost and rubbed her consolingly on the shoulder without answering. The fear on Anna's face broke my heart.

"I am so *tired* of all of you," I sighed wearily and put my head in my hands. I felt Gunther's strong arms wrap around me and his hand brush through my hair. "Everything is a struggle, a conflict, a disagreement. And I have to say I'm just so tired of it all."

"Hey!" Cama squeaked as Gunther accidentally dislodged her.

"Oh, sorry, Cama," Gunther murmured. He removed his hand from my hair and dropped it to my back. "Honey, what can I do?"

"Is there anything anyone can do?" I asked him. "Is there anything that anyone can do to make all of this *stop*?"

No one responded.

CHAPTER 11

"SHE *CLAIMED* THAT?" GUNTHER ASKED ME, astonished, after I took him into my private living area and detailed what Fortuna had told me. "*Just you, though? Not the two of us?*"

"What, are you *disappointed* that you weren't singled out as a circus-killer, too?" I asked him archly. "We could stroll back over to Fortuna's tent and get *you* a reading. Maybe you're destined to accomplish something just as awful."

He didn't look offended, only thoughtful. "And she wouldn't tell you how or why it transpired, just that it did?"

"She was really close-mouthed about it, which was strange, to tell you the truth," I said as I flopped onto the bed. "She was so persistent about needing to give me a reading when I went in there, and then when she did, she just dropped a bomb and suddenly wouldn't say any more."

"Maybe she's scared of affecting your choice?"

"Isn't the whole point of getting a prophetic reading to influence somebody's opinion?" I laughed more from nervousness than anything else. "I mean, why bother to get a reading at all if it's not meant to influence something?"

Gunther didn't laugh, and he didn't respond. He just sat leaning against my makeup desk looking lost in thought. "It's clever," he said eventually.

"What's clever?" I asked.

"Before you got that reading from Fortuna, had it ever occurred to you that you *could* dismantle both of the circuses? That it was even a choice you could make?"

"The first thought anyone put into my head when I became ringmaster was that a deficiency on my part could kill everyone here," I pointed out. "And you took the walls down, so it feels like you kind of—"

"No, listen to what I'm saying—"

"Don't cut me off and don't talk to me like a child, Gunther," I snapped, exasperated. Gunther looked startled and somewhat hurt. I groaned.

"I'm sorry. I don't know why I just did that. I'm just tired. You know, I *really* thought when the Witches' Council was taken out of the picture, we could have some peace."

"Just because they're less powerful doesn't mean they're gone. They *do* still rule the paranormal world. But I understand, Charlotte." Gunther smiled. "I was simply trying to point out that the circuses, and the people *within* the circuses? Those are really two different things." I frowned. "You don't agree?"

"I don't think I *disagree*, but I just never considered them separate before."

"We set up the circuses, at least before we found out about this whole fight between the gods thing, to help people hide from the mistreatment perpetrated by the Witches' Council."

"So you're suggesting that without the Witches' Council persecuting people...the circuses are no longer needed?" I asked thoughtfully. Gunther nodded. "If hiding is no longer necessary, why is Ms. Elkins pushing to move the circuses to the ringmaster realm?"

"That's a good question," Gunther shrugged. "It's a question I don't believe we know the answer to yet. There is one thing, though, I'm not sure you're aware of."

"What's that?"

"Norns can be both malicious and compassionate. Some single norns can be both," Gunther explained and my jaw dropped. "When we learned about norns in school, they pointed out that benevolent norns could be kind and protective. Malevolent ones could cause destructive and disastrous events. The point is, though, that they have within them the power to cause both."

"We've been assuming all this time that Ms. Elkins is benevolent. Are you saying you don't think she is?"

"I suspect Mina World would disagree that she is," Gunther pointed out. "To Mina, Ms. Elkins brought about events that cursed her and all she had been working toward for *hundreds* of years."

"But Mina was wrong," I argued.

"I doubt *Mina* feels that way," Gunther replied.

It was well past midnight, and the warm Texas sun had given way to a bite in the air. After

Gunther and I spoke, I had excused myself from my yurt and walked out past the hordes of people examining my sins, Gunther's mistakes, and all the things they felt we should do next.

I just needed to be alone for a bit, get some air.

I found myself walking slowly on the path between the two circuses and my parents' house. From the path I could see the glow from the animal shelter, and for a moment the stall full of pups was a tempting escape.

"I *don't* know what to do," I grumbled to the tree along the path. Ironically, it was the tree that Cama had waited in when we found her months ago. "I don't even know what I'm expected to be thinking about doing. It feels never-ending."

"It is never-ending," a gruff voice murmured to me from the shadows at the base of the tree. Wait—trees talk now? "For long as you exist, resolutions of how to move forward will always come again once you step, child. It is inevitable."

"Who's there?" I demanded as I hopped back from the tree. I bent my knees into a defensive posture that would likely be worthless against anything that assailed me, all things considered. But it made me feel better.

"Your heart is still pure, child, and you still have nothing to fear from me," the voice whispered roughly and the obscured woman materialized from the trunk of the thick tree. I couldn't see her features. It was as if she was wrapped in writhing darkness.

Cama's mother.

Great.

Just what I needed.

"I do sense, however, that your heart is burdened," she hissed, gliding toward me. "In my embrace, child, that would *all* disappear," the darkly beautiful reaper whispered. She opened her arms wide. "All decisions would be made, all matters that vex you would fall away. Responsibility would become someone else's burden. Do you wish to lay them down?"

"Step back," I ordered her as she crossed toward me.

"Did you *not* ask for this all to stop?" the woman asked me, her arms still outstretched. She moved ever closer.

I gulped.

"That's *not* what I meant," I told her. The light along the path caused gentle rays to pass through her dark body in flashing streaks. "I'm not ready to die, thanks. I appreciate the offer, though," I told her with as much polite nonchalance as I could muster while being terrified, even though I really *didn't* appreciate the offer.

Like, at all.

I could feel my heart thud in my chest.

"Surely you understood when you spoke that *death* is what you sought?" the woman halted and tilted her head, inspecting me curiously. "Life is about striving, *movement*. When you ask for this to stop? You ask for *life* to stop."

"Yeah, again, *not* what I meant," I told her unequivocally. I tiptoed back slowly. "So, I'm good. Nothing to see here. Sorry to have disturbed you."

"Words have *force*." Her voice snapped and lightning blazed in the sky.

"Look, I take it back!" I stepped back again.

"Good," the woman...smiled? I guess. Just like that, the menace I felt from her was gone, and I tried to breathe.

"Awesome," I choked out, and I tried to smile.

"I get no satisfaction out of reaping the fragile-willed. So much lost potential."

"Well, *that's* kind of rude," I muttered, and suddenly I remembered—a second too late to keep my trap shut and my snarky comments to myself—who I was speaking to. "I'm sorry, I didn't mean any disrespect for who you are or what you do—"

"You do not *understand* who I am or what I do," she rasped without judgment. "But that is as it should be, truly, and it does not annoy or disturb me. What concerns me is whether you will figure out what you must do in time to do it."

Oh, awesome.

Another supernatural being here to tell me what I have to do.

Because I don't have enough of those.

"That's what I was out here thinking about... goddess...um, ma'am," I told her, puzzled about what I was even to call her.

"You may call me Shadow, Charlotte Astley of the Magical Midway, Charlotte Astley of the Makepeace Circus, Charlotte Astley of Mickwac, Texas. Though you are *all* those things," she rasped, "I am simply the shadow of life. I am that which all must drop behind them, all things concealed from the light. I know them."

I wasn't sure what to say to that.

"I made sure that the scroll would be put in your hands," Shadow said as she moved forward. "You have done nothing with it. It does not even cross your mind."

"Well, my husband put two gods in a box, a

bunch of cats are missing, one of the Witches' Council is here and another is on her way—"

"All meaningless," she said and lightning crashed through the clear, starry sky. "Only the scroll matters, and the choice is still yours."

"You mean mine and Gunther's," I told her.

"The choice is yours," she echoed, and lightning burst through the clear sky again.

Shadow and I looked at one another until I heard strong, leathery wings flapping and a chittering squeal of "Mama!"

"Hello, my love," the undulating shadow cooed as Cama wrapped her wings about the woman's head. "Are your aunt and uncle suitably distressed at their predicament?"

"I haven't talked to them but every time I fly by they look *really* miserable," Cama assured her. "I don't think they thought Gunther could do what he did. But then he *did*. And I don't think even Gunther thought he could do what he did. And then there they were! And you know how Aunt Maggie *hates* the color blue."

"Indeed, I do," Shadow murmured, cuddling the bat. Turning to me, she held Cama out and the bat flew from her ghostly hand back into my hair. "You have taken good care of my daughter."

"It was nothing, really," I said through

clenched teeth while the bat skittered around my head looking for a spot. "She really just kind of hangs out and takes care of herself, more or less. And she hasn't killed anyone, so that was good."

"Death bats are shunned because death leads to the renewal," Shadow said and the dark swirled around her faster. "You were singled out because you do not fear. Do *not* fail us," the woman's whisper faded and the black smoke vanished.

"I'm really impressed," Cama said. She rushed in front of me and confronted me. The cute bat eyed me up and down. "Mama jumped out at you and you *didn't* even pee in your pants!"

~

"I fear," I complained. I walked up the stairs to my parents' house. "Chosen because I don't *fear*. I don't know what kind of hogwash that was—"

"Charlotte, is that you?" Mom called from somewhere inside the house when I cleared the back door. I called back and heard her ask my father to stop whatever he was doing to come see me.

"I just had a visit from death," I told my mother when she joined me in the kitchen. "*Not surprisingly, my mouth is super dry. Do you have any iced tea?"

"Let me get you some." She opened the refrigerator and poured me a towering glass. "Was this visit metaphorical or did something happen, or—"

"I *wish* it was metaphorical," I confessed.

As I savored the tea in the kitchen and allowed my heart rate to return to normal, I disclosed to my parents all that had been taking place on the Magical Midway (and the Makepeace Circus), climaxing in a report of my communication with Shadow on the trail. As I concluded, they looked at me with compassion.

"It sounds like you have a monumental decision to make," Dad spoke with a somber smile.

"I don't even know what decision I'm *supposed* to be making," I told him, my expression also gloomy.

"Well, you are Maggie's representative, Charlotte," Mom told me as she refilled my glass from the pitcher. "I think Gunther's been taken out of the equation, at least as far as some of the spirits are concerned, because he's Eiggam's agent now. I don't believe it's a snub against Gunther or any judgment on your relationship, dear."

Well, I hadn't expected it was, but *now* mom had me concerned about Gunther and me, too. I bit my lip.

"Oh, stop that, Charlotte, I meant nothing by that," Mom chastised me when she caught my expression.

"Gunther's point about Ms. Elkins was fairly insightful," my father told me. "The norns do seem to have their own agenda, what with the whole *spinning the fates of men* thing. Just because she's influenced you up until now doesn't mean you should continue listening to her."

"Well, Gunther's dad definitely thinks I should ignore her."

"Roland always had a problem with lofty pronouncements, no matter who they came from," Dad said wryly.

I turned to Dad in surprise. "I thought you didn't pay much attention to the Magical Midway, Dad?"

"I didn't talk to my brother often, but I *talked* to him, Charlotte," Dad told me quickly, smiling again. "Regardless of whether I preferred to be connected with the circus, the circus is our family's legacy. I had a duty to stay updated."

The three of us sat quietly together. Well, Dad and I sat, and Mom busied herself in that way

Mom had. It astonished me that Dad had kept in contact with Uncle Phil enough to know some of the ins and outs I was dealing with, and I again wondered why they were kept from me for so many years. It wasn't a debate I wanted to have right now, though. It didn't really matter anymore.

But it occurred to me that Dad would have been so much better qualified than I was to be ringmaster.

"Why do you think you weren't chosen?" I asked Dad.

"Because it was your turn," Dad responded with a shrug.

"You don't think it was any more than that?"

"Charlotte, you and Gunther are *plainly* made for each other," Mom said as she distractedly wiped off the already clean table with a wet rag. "How do you expect you and that boy would've gotten together if you were just visiting once a year for a week?"

"You don't think we would've moved to the circus if Dad had become the ringmaster?" I asked her, surprised.

My parents looked at one another, sharing a glance that held meaning I didn't recognize. Finally, my father turned from my mother and looked at me, shaking his head. "Look at what we've built here, Charlotte, how many lives we save." A dog howled from the kennels as if to clarify his point. "Someone would've had to take care of things here. That would have left your mother and you."

"In any case, I don't think that ever would've happened," my mother continued. "Part of the reason we're so successful at what we do is that your dad can talk to the animals we rescue."

"It's true," Dad agreed with Mom.

"We wouldn't have given up what we do here, saving these wonderful creatures. And to do that as well as we do it, your father needed to be *here*. I don't think he would ever have been the ringmaster, Charlotte—and if he had been, he would have been miserable. I'm very glad we never put him in the position of having to make a choice between his calling and his duty."

"Everything worked out the way it was meant to," Dad smiled. "The circus was always intended for you, Charlie."

As I sat at my parents' table, I wondered if their confidence in destiny was right.

And if it was—was I truly was the person who would wipe out the circuses forever?

CHAPTER 12

"WHAT THE EVER-LOVING—" I DEMANDED AS I trudged back toward the blue box and the two circuses. We had many people living in the two circuses, but the crowd size around the estranged supernatural couple had more than tripled.

"I hope you got enough air," Tabitha said. She walked up beside me as I inspected the crowd in confusion. "Because if you didn't, you apparently won't find it in that crowd."

"Who *are* all these people?" I asked her.

"Gunther said they're a bunch of paranormals from all over. Apparently, soothsayers and psychics from all and sundry have foretold that you will do something ludicrous in the next day or so, and they all want to see it. Or something."

"Scout?" I caught sight of a tall, athletic man about ten feet in front of me. A group of fierce-looking, bearded, brown-haired men swathed in black leather surrounded him. "Scout Trout, is that *you?*"

"Charlotte Astley," the Cavemaster of the werebears smiled broadly. He turned, ran over, and engulfed me into the quintessential bear hug. It was so tight that I struggled to inhale.

"No armor!" I gasped. Scout dropped me and peered down with apprehension. "What are you doing here?" I choked as I steadied myself on my feet.

"You are a sister of the bear clan," Scout said matter-of-factly. "We take that seriously, and we felt you might need us." The men behind him nodded as they stared at me. "Besides, *all* leaders of all clans are making their way here for the big occasion."

"What do you mean *all?*"

Scout replied. "I mean all. The werebears may be the first you've seen," he said as he craned his neck to survey the crowds. "But we were far from the first to come. The elves, gnomes, centaurs, werecreatures of all types. All expect that within the next three days, things will change. They have all been compelled by whatever spirits guide them to come here. To see you."

"There won't be any vampires or anything, will there?"

All the werebears hissed in reply to my question.

"Those abominations would not dare come," Scout said gravely. "Not with the wolves in attendance, clearly."

"Clearly," I said, even though nothing was clear to me. I skimmed around and tried to distinguish those new to the area. I was thankful that all seem to be in their humanoid forms as they milled about presenting themselves to one another. "Has anyone been told what I'm supposed to do?" I inquired confidently.

Scout looked appalled at my question. He leaned forward and whispered in my ear. "You don't know?"

I stepped back from his grim expression and swung back to Tabitha. "Have you talked to Bob? Do the lares guards have this under control?"

"I have talked to Bob," Tabitha replied, and she pointed to the other side of the crowded clearing where Bob stood. His cloaks were disheveled and his face shrouded in a five o'clock shadow, as if he hadn't had time to pay attention to himself in days. His expression made clear that he was floundering. "He says there are too many people here, and the humans will no doubt come to investigate."

"Yeah, I was thinking the same thing," I murmured as I tried to count how many people were milling about the field.

"Can't you just have Gunther undo what he did?"

"He didn't do it alone," I explained her. I kept counting.

"Okay, can't you *both* just undo what you *both* did?" Tabitha restated. "I get that hugging and kissing is an essential part of a relationship, Charlotte, but someone's going to notice this is going on. Even if someone doesn't come to investigate because it looks suspicious? If I was a human, and I glanced over here, I would assume the circuses were open for business."

"It's more than the kissing and hugging, Tabitha."

"Well, clearly. I'm not a moron, Charlotte."

I blushed furiously.

"What I mean is," I told her while trying not to look embarrassed, "the power was in our shield and the confines of the circuses. That force now contains the two gods so their energy doesn't infect everyone the way it did."

"Are they actually gods?" Tabitha asked.

"Honestly, I have no idea, it's just the clearest word to use at the moment." Tabitha gave me a protracted, intense look. "What?"

"Go talk to them," she replied. "This scene is starting to spiral out of control."

"Starting?" I laughed.

I thought about going to get Gunther, but everybody had built up over and over in the past twenty-four hours that the choice (whatever decision that was) would be mine only, and so I didn't.

As I stepped up to the blue cube a hush fell over the watching crowd as if I had just announced a tight rope walk high in the air. Hundreds of eyes followed when I reached my palm out toward the bright wall. I smiled as my hand moved through.

My smile didn't last long. On the other side of the wall, Maggie grabbed my open hand and jerked me into the cube with her and Eiggam. I stumbled inside and unceremoniously landed on my rump.

"You will let me out of here!" Maggie growled at me as she stooped down next to me and clutched my face. "In all my years of existence I have never been so humiliated in my entire life. Locked in a box by a *child!*"

I had met little girl Maggie. I had met sultry Maggie. I'd met funny Maggie and mystical Maggie. This was a Maggie I hadn't met, and this Maggie was so furious her stare felt like it had physical pressure to it.

"I'm not a child," I told her shakily. I leaned against the wall and pushed myself up and away from her grasp. "I will not let either of you out until we talk. You made everybody in both circuses lose their minds! What was Gunther *supposed* to do?"

"We *have* talked, you and I," Maggie replied indignantly. "And he *could* have just asked us *nicely* to rein it in, you know."

"Seriously?"

"Well, did either of you *try* it?" she demanded haughtily.

"Outside these walls, every paranormal leader

has come here because I'm expected to make some kind of judgment that affects everybody, and I don't even know what it is," I told her and began pacing. "Death has stopped me and told that she wants me to do something—"

"My sister Shadow always wants witches to do something," Maggie said dismissively. "She never gets what she wants, so she won't be very disappointed when you don't do it. Don't bother about it. I doubt she'll slay you for it."

That was reassuring.

"Do you know what she wants from me?"

"Let me out of here and I'll tell you," Maggie said casually with a shrug.

"Yeah, *that's* not going to happen," I stammered as I paced. Raising my eyes to Eiggam, who leaned in the corner observing the two of us, I asked him, "And what do *you* think about all this? Are you going to threaten me to let you out, too?"

"Nope," he responded.

I looked at him curiously. It stunned me that he could see me at all, since the two of them hadn't previously been able to see each other's representatives. "Why not?"

"You don't owe me anything," Eiggam told me.

"I have the scroll," I told him.

No answer.

"Doesn't that mean anything to you?"

"It means you have the scroll," Eiggam replied, and he shrugged. "Sometimes, the truth is just what it is, Ms. Astley. That you're in here and not with the scroll tells me where your priorities lie."

"What is *that* supposed to mean?" I asked him, but he didn't acknowledge my question at all. "You know what? Forget it. I don't care."

"You do," he stated.

"Do not," I responded.

"Children," Eiggam said, rolling his eyes.

"Aren't the two of you tired of fighting?" I asked the two mighty gods in a fit of pique. "You're husband and wife! You must've loved each other once."

Both Maggie and Eiggam looked aggrieved at my remark.

"Well, of course we *worship* one another," Maggie told me. "This isn't about an absence of love. It's about a paucity of respect, and a scarcity of *appreciation*."

"It's simply a disagreement," Eiggam shrugged, speaking far more plainly than his wife.

"It's a fight that's breaking our world *apart*, and I can't accept the two of you are happy being without one another for hundreds of years," I said, pleading with the two of them. "Conspiring against each other. Hurting each other. No one's happy here, *everybody* is fighting all the time, and that means *nothing* is staying the same and nothing is moving forward. Nothing that *either one of you want* is taking place, so *how* is this working?"

"I want to win," Maggie scoffed.

"As do I," Eiggam agreed.

"How is it winning if you're both alone, and our world just keeps fighting?" I demanded. I pointed out at the sea of faces beyond the blue barrier light. "Or if one of you wins and the other is broken? And now you've made Gunther and me opposite polarities in a battle we don't even understand. I don't want to lose my husband because the two of you are in an argument!"

"Well, of course you don't, dear," Maggie told me, her smug expression softening as tears filled my eyes. "Your Gunther is a good man. My husband wouldn't have chosen him as a champion if he was undeserving. Even though he plundered him from our party and that should be considered cheating," Maggie scowled at Eiggam. "You should be proud of him."

"Proud?" I asked her, shocked. "The lawgiver rings have determined we're unredeemable!"

"Oh, pish," Maggie replied as she waved my concern aside. "The lawgiver ring turned black because Gunther became Eiggam's champion. You didn't need its power on top of ours, so it went away."

"They were the last two rings!"

"So make more," Maggie nodded then. She glanced over at Eiggam and the two of them shook their heads as if I was a dull child that didn't get it. "You and Gunther are equals now. Doesn't that make you happy? My husband is an exceptional judge of character, you know," she revealed.

Eiggam nodded, and I felt like I was caught in *The Twilight Zone*.

"You know, he previously chose Mina—never mind, forget I said anything." I exhaled and stopped pacing. "Forget all else. Gunther and I *love* each other, and even when we fight? We *still* love each other. There's *no* fight so extraordinary that *eradicating* the other person makes it worth winning."

"How sweet," Maggie whispered. Eiggam coughed.

"Please stop this, both of you," I implored.

"You said Gunther should have asked. I'm asking —please, end this. I searched all my life for Gunther, and now that I found him...I...*Please* don't use the two of us as puppets in a dispute that will destroy the two of you, too. Because even if one of you wins, the other still loses everything. And then no one will win."

Silence descended as the two powerful beings stared at one another. It was as if they had never thought about where this all would end.

And they call us fools.

"Your agent is wise," Eiggam said as he looked humbly at his wife.

"Well, of *course* she is, that's why I chose her," Maggie snapped and crossed her arms.

"Maggie!" I shrieked.

"Sorry," she murmured.

"Can we please stop the fighting? Please? I just want to start my life with my husband without continually looking over my shoulder in dread that someone's coming to kill me. Or that I'll be taken over and will hurt him," I told them, weepy emotions catching in my throat. "Please, I'm begging you..."

"Oh, fine, if you both stop crying!" Eiggam flung up his hands. "That's all these paranormals need is to look in this box and see two gods and their two champions sniveling like fools!"

"Two champions?" I asked. I shifted around to see Gunther in the corner behind me, tears flowing down his face. "Oh, I...um...hi," I told him, mortified that he'd seen my outpouring of emotion.

Look, I'm kind of stoic.

It was an embarrassing outpouring.

"Hi," he whispered and rushed across the box to take me in his arms.

The crowd all cooed as the two gods and the two champions snogged in the big blue box.

"I can't believe that's all it took," I whispered to Gunther as we pulled back.

"Love, forgiveness...those are not simple things," Gunther told me. We turned to face Maggie and Eiggam, who were now wrapped in each other's arms. "So, what now?"

"We are going to take a vacation," Maggie announced. "The two of you still have some decisions to make."

"Wait, no...I mean, you're back together again.

So, stability comes back to the world and progress and—"

"We cannot take back the power that we gave you," he shrugged again. "We have our own power, of course, but what we have given you cannot be returned to us. It's yours."

"I don't understand," I told him with alarm.

"We hope that you'll let us out of this box," Maggie told me warmly. "But what you do with this energy, that's entirely up to the two of you. We can't take it back. Those were the rules we agreed to."

"So change the rules," Gunther told her.

"That is how all this started," Eiggam responded. "Is that truly what you wish us to do? Debate the change of rules?"

Gunther and I both shook our head simultaneously.

"You have the scroll," Maggie said. She and Eiggam walked to the side of the cube and tapped on the wall. "Do with the energy what you will. You have both brought us back together, so clearly you are wise."

"Yeah, you know, I don't feel like I'm all that wise. I mean, we had like a five minute conversation here, and I begged a bit, and you agreed, but I don't really feel like I did much—"

"We have ended our disagreement not because of what you said here, but because of what you and Gunther have done since the two of you met," Eiggam said. He knocked on the wall again and raised his eyebrow. "What you said here only brought out what my love and I had already been feeling since the two of you came to power."

"When you think about it, Eiggam choosing Gunther really made this fully possible, so you two really didn't do all *that* much," Maggie said as she whacked on the wall with a fist. "Now, now, children, I'm getting a little claustrophobic in here. Let's take the cube down before the gods get a bit more testy, shall we?"

"But I have questions—"

"Drop the walls, girl, and go talk to your cat," Maggie said through clenched teeth. "I have a beach to go lay on, and I gave you the guardian so I wouldn't have to be involved with these petty concerns."

"Charlotte, I think we should…" Gunther grabbed my hand.

I gave Maggie one last pleading look, and sighed. I took Gunther's other hand and we looked into each other's eyes, concentrating on returning the power to where it apparently belonged. I felt a lurch as the box exploded and settled back to protect what it had been protecting all the years before Gunther had condensed it to jail the impetuous gods.

When I opened my eyes, Maggie and Eiggam were gone.

I laid my head on Gunther's chest and heard the telltale clank. He held me as tight as he could while I wept.

CHAPTER 13

"YOU SHOULD HAVE LISTENED," MS. ELKINS SAID AS she crocheted. "Now, you're down here with no beings to advise you, all this power left in your hands, and you could sneeze and unwittingly destroy the world. I hope you're happy."

"Stop being so melodramatic," Roland told the norn. Ms. Elkins clicked her tongue and grunted.

"Where's Samson?" I asked Tabitha. "Have any of you seen Samson?" Tabitha shook her head.

"Can't you reach him with that mind meld thing?"

"I don't know," I responded in a half-choked whisper. I felt adrift, like a sealed up test-tube of water drifting in a vast ocean. I was the same as all around me, but cut off. Alone.

"So, try?" Tabitha asked me and held out her hands. I glanced at her, my eyes wide. Hers narrowed. "Hold it together, Charlotte. You will not sneeze and wreck the world. That old woman is just trying to shock you."

"Oh ho, look at the know-it-all human," Ms. Elkins said aloud. Everybody in the area turned toward her.

"You've been alive how long?" Tabitha asked her.

"Longer than you can conceive—"

"So, in all those years you've been hatching this whole thing, Ms. Elkins, you never made a contingency plan for something like this?" Tabitha neared the old woman. Ms. Elkins hands ceased moving in her lap and her eyes jerked up to scowl at Tabitha. "I haven't even hit forty yet, and I could have divined this would turn into a mess."

"You smug little—"

"Stop it," I told Ms. Elkins wearily. My tone was subdued, and even I could hear the hopelessness echo in it.

"Is everything all right?" Samantha Goodfellow asked no one in particular when she entered the dorm yurt. Sarah Stevens whispered in her ear and pointed toward Tabitha, who towered over the norn. "Tabitha, are you all right, dear?"

"I'm fine, Priestess," Tabitha told her politely. She did not take her eyes from the norn. Kyle and Aidan looked back and forth between the women. Fortuna pushed past them.

"No more readings!" I called out at her. My heated demand caused people in the room to jump nervously. "If there's another thing doomed to fall on my head, just let it fall. I don't want to know about the next train that will hit me before it's expected to pull into the station."

Fortuna stopped in the center of the room and looked at me. Her expression was one of faint disappointment.

Samantha Goodfellow crossed over toward the table and sat down beside Kyle and Aidan with an "oomph." "It astounds me frequently when I visit your circus to look around and see how many human beings are within these canvas walls." She patted Kyle on the arm.

"I'm not human," Kyle told her.

"You are, dear," Samantha Goodfellow smiled at the centaur. "You spent most of your life in our world. You were even one of our champions, fighting for the mortal notion of law and order. Just because you have hooves and a tail sometimes doesn't make you any less human."

"But humans are a species," Aidan pointed out.

"Homo sapiens are a species," Tabitha disagreed. "The word *human* can be an adjective."

"*Wise man*," Kyle muttered.

"What?" I asked him.

"Homo sapiens. It's Latin for wise man," Kyle told me.

"Right, and paranormal...para is from Greek. It means contrary to—"

"In Italian it means to ward off," Tabitha disagreed.

"So we are contrary to normalcy or we actively ward off normalcy," I said with resentment. "Thanks for this English lesson, folks. It's really made me feel better." I grabbed a pillow from the couch and clutched it around my head. The pillow smelled like popcorn.

"I think it's more complicated than that, Charlotte, but none of us are etymologists," Tabitha frowned. "You really are twined tight today, aren't you?"

I peeked out into the room and glared at her.

"I didn't mean for anyone to read too much into my thought, I confess," Samantha Goodfellow said pleasantly. "This is just quite a balanced group. Half human," she said as she pointed to herself, Sarah, and Tabitha. "We also have half paranormal," she continued, pointing to me, Fortuna and Roland. "And yet Roland is the only paranormal in this room who has never been a part of the human world."

I looked around, studying the group. "This isn't exactly *balanced*, though, Ms. Goodfellow," I told her. "There's no human in this room that hasn't been a part of the paranormal, at least a little."

"Roland hasn't been wholly apart from it since his death, either, though, has he?" the portly woman pointed out. "It's just fascinating to see this balance, that's all. Maybe what Maggie and Eiggam did was essential after all."

Fortuna continued studying at me quietly.

I sneezed and sank my head back under the pillow.

Balance.

That word nagged at me.

"Charlotte?" Gunther whispered, and I dragged my head up and my awareness back to the room. "Are you okay?"

"Did you find the cats?" I asked him without responding.

"The…um, which ones?"

"Any of them?"

"No," he shook his head and gazed across the room. "How are things going here?"

"Balanced," I told him, and he turned back to me. "How are things going out there?"

"Bizarrely fine," Gunther said, sounding bewildered. "Almost everyone who's in charge of anyone in the paranormal world is here now. They're all enjoying food, drink, and each other as if this was one big celebration. They seem calm," Gunther frowned. "It's kind of baffling, actually."

"*Why* is that word nagging at me so much?" I asked him with irritation. "Ever since Ms. Goodfellow mentioned how balanced this room was with humans and paranormals, it's like she tickled some itch in my head I can't scratch."

"Maybe it's Devana?"

"What about Devana?"

"She used to say that *all* the time when she first arrived here," Gunther reminded me. Ms. Elkins began pushing herself up out of her chair to the right of us. "That she served nothing but the balance."

"The balance of what?" I asked him, trying to remember.

"She never really said more than that, not that I remember," he said. He spotted Ms. Elkins, her eyes narrow, trudging toward us. "I think Ms. Elkins is about to intrude further."

"Don't," I told her when she sat down close to us. "Whatever you have to say, just don't. I need a break for a few minutes to get my head together, and I don't want to hear anything from you right now."

The old woman reached out and slammed me in the face. Her ring clanged loudly against my armor. I was, once again, an impenetrable fortress of one, but the indignity of what she just did flared a fire of anger within me. I gawked at her in outrage, and suddenly my eyes narrowed fiercely. I had just about enough of the norn.

"Don't be impolite," Ms. Elkins snapped at me.

"Don't hit me," I cautioned her.

"Or you'll *what?*" she asked, crossing her arms.

"The perimeter is back up now," I said. I leaned forward and looked up at her. "That means all the old rules are back in place, and I'm the ringmaster here. I can evict you with a sustained thought, old woman."

"I'd like to see you try!" Ms. Elkins shouted at me. "You never bound me here in the first place!"

So I did. I didn't even bother standing up to do it.

And she disappeared.

Gunther stared at me slack-jawed as his father floated around the room, peals of laughter ringing from the ghost.

"*Ejected* her?" Devana asked, suspicious. Scout stood beside her looking interested.

"Look, I know that she raised you, and all, but I'm really losing patience with people treating me like a fool they can push around. And whacking me just set me off," I revealed. I leaned against the kitchen counter. "Shield or not, it just isn't cool."

"You *banished* her from the circus? *A norn?*"

"Ms. Elkins, yes. Banished, barred, banned. Whoosh. Gone."

"But *how* did you have the power to do so?"

"Dunno," I shrugged. Roland Makepeace acted out with tremendous dramatic flair what had taken place for his wife, Gerda, and daughter, Anna, behind us. "Don't care. I will not be assaulted every time I turn around by an ancient woman with a god complex."

"But I—"

"Look, I'm sure she's fine," I cut off the shocked huntress witch. "We have other things we need to deal with. I need to ask you something. You told me once—well, more than once—that you served the balance. What did you mean by that?"

Samantha Goodfellow and Sarah Stevens had been deep in conversation with Tabitha. At my question, all three stopped talking and turned to listen.

"My kind seeks to keep the world in balance, Charlotte," Devana explained quietly, her voice taking on a breathy cadence. "The world runs well when it is balanced. I am the unity in a world of opposites."

"I don't understand what that means," I conceded. "I mean, I understand the words. But in practicality, what does it mean, exactly?"

"The world, human and paranormal both, values opposition. Right and wrong, life and death, success and failure. In nature," she beamed, "there is no such thing. There are no right and wrong trees—there are large and small trees, ripe fruit and unripe fruit, blooming flowers and ones that have yet to bloom. But these are not opposites, as each has its purpose and its promise. A small tree does not feel secondary to a more substantial one, it only is what it is."

Everyone in the room stared at the stately woman as she spoke. Scout's eyes glowed as he listened to his former love, admiration written across his face.

"Do you understand? I am the unity in a world of opposites," Devana repeated. "Well, not just me. Many work for the balance. Some aren't even aware if it. It is in unanimity that we are fully realized, Charlotte. Until that day, there are those of us that work to hold the balance intended for this world."

"Having and not having arise together, difficult and easy complement each other," Kyle whispered. *"Long and short contrast each other, high and low rest upon each other—"*

"Front and back follow one another," Aidan finished.

"Yes," Devana smiled and nodded, sounding pleased that the couple seemed to understand her.

"What was that?" I asked them.

"Lao Tzu," Kyle told me. "He was a Chinese philosopher."

"He also said, '*At the center of your being you have the answer; you know who you are and you know what you want*'," Aidan said to me, his eyes sparkling with power.

The etymology lesson had given way to a philosophy lecture.

"The dude also said, '*when nothing is done, nothing is left undone*'," Tabitha said wryly. "So, should we just forget about all of this stuff and play some Mahjong, then?"

Tabitha was right, philosophy would not solve this problem. And man, I *hated* philosophy in college. I took one class and dropped it three weeks in once I recognized there were no right answers.

This situation wasn't a class I could drop, no matter how much I wanted to.

CHAPTER 14

"I'D ASK YOU FOR A HUG, BUT IT WOULD JUST BE A reminder we're wrapped in these invisible suits of armor *again*," I told Gunther. We were wandering along the periphery of the circuses. He had taken me out among the clans that had turned up while I was hiding my face in a cushion. After I greeted everyone, he proposed a walk where it was quiet.

"I am glad that Maggie and Eiggam left," Gunther said serenely. He gently brushed my hand. "Even if we are still opposites as far as power is concerned, I'm less worried about... doing something I don't want to do. With them off someplace else? It just feels safer, I think."

"I was worried about that, too," I conceded.

We walked beyond the border into the shadowy fields between the circuses and the animal shelter. "I don't think I would have been able to live with myself if I'd hurt you."

"You could never hurt me on purpose, Charlotte," Gunther smiled, his golden hair shining in the moonlight.

"I'm glad you know that," I told him. And I was glad. Sometimes, Gunther's confidence in me was overwhelming—and I often thought it was undeserved. He'd been through so much since he met me.

"Stop that," he admonished.

"What? Gain telepathy, did we?" I told him, pointing out the fact that our lawgiver rings (and the psychic bond we had because of them) were gone.

"Charlotte Makepeace, if you think I need to be in your head to know what you're thinking, you're *greatly* mistaken," Gunther said wryly. He reached out to caress my cheek. I shuddered involuntarily as he said what, in the ordinary human world for years and years, would have been my married name. "I don't think you are as stoic as you assume you are. At least not to me."

I exhaled. "You think more of me than you should, sometimes. By the way," I told him, pointing a finger at his chest. "We haven't spoken about whether I would take your name, so that's some *serious* assumption, buddy."

Gunther looked at me, silent. He seemed hurt. "What?"

"I just...I didn't...I—"

"Look, I'm not mad," I told him, waving away his apprehension.

"I didn't mean to—"

"In the modern world, though, women don't *automatically* take the husband's name. I'm not property, you know," I explained to him, even though in some ways that's absolutely what I felt like. Not because of anything Gunther did or said, but because my life had been governed first by my father, then by the circus and Maggie. Gunther assuming I would take his name looked like another indignity in some ways.

Even though having his name sent quivers down my spine.

Look, I'm a feminist and all, but there's something to be said for old-fashioned tradition, too.

Gunther nudged me into his arms and apologized for assuming. I shrugged it off and fell with a clink into his arms. "I'm sorry for snapping. I think I'm just—what was it Tabitha said? Twined a little tight today?"

I could sense that Gunther nodded. After a short time, he cleared his throat. "What is it you *need*?" Gunther asked, his voice soft against my hair.

"This hug is good," I murmured and breathed in Gunther's scent. He squeezed his light embrace into a real hug and kissed me on the cheek. Pulling back, he inclined his head as he examined me, his eyes meeting mine. My stomach plummeted at the serious expression on his face. "What? What is it?"

"I don't mean right *now*, Charlotte," Gunther smiled as if something amused him. "I mean for the future. Our future, the circuses' future. When you look ahead, what do you see when you see our life together? *Do* you see a life for us?"

I didn't answer. I didn't know how.

"If you could make anything happen, anything *you* want," Gunther continued, "what would it be?"

"I don't really think about the future, Gunther," I told him. I stared off toward the horizon and detected the first streaks of daybreak. "We have to move."

"Charlotte, I think we need to talk about this,"

Gunther protested as I grabbed his arm. "I've been very clear about what I want. But you…" His voice trailed off.

Pulling Gunther toward the circus, I reminded him of the day and night cycles that ruled me. "Just so you know? *This* is what I think about. The sun's coming up, I have to get back to the circus. The cats are missing, I have to find them. There's no room in my head for anything else."

"I know, but those are situations to be handled, not—"

"I don't have the *energy* to dream, Gunther," I declared as we walked back into the circus and turned to watch the sunrise. "We step from one calamity to another."

"What if we didn't?" Gunther asked me gently.

"Well, *that* would be magic," I confessed. "And it's the *one* magic we don't seem to possess."

The circus was hushed while Gunther and I wandered back silently toward my yurt in the brisk early morning air. People were strewn everywhere as if there had been an all-night party that just ran out of steam, and loud snoring echoed from all corners. Our newest arrivals had traveled overnight, and the meets and greets had clearly taken their toll on the energy.

I smiled as I stepped over a werebear snoring in the middle of the path. His head rested casually on a werelion's belly.

"Look," Gunther whispered. He pointed to a hay bale. Scout Trout, the chief of the werebears, rested peacefully with Devana wrapped in his arms. Their faces both had faint smiles. I got a warm flush of delight for the solitary huntress witch. Maybe she hadn't been hanging out with Scout *just* for an in with the werebears after all.

Devana shifted in her sleep, and her arm fell across Scout's powerful chest.

"Maybe we should take a cue from everyone and go get some sleep ourselves," Gunther pointed out. "It's been a very long night."

"What about the cats?"

"Which ones?"

"All of them," I told Gunther as we tiptoed into my yurt and I yawned. "You and I don't *have* to sleep. Shouldn't we be looking for them?"

Gunther's face took on a distant look, and he shook his head. "I still don't believe they are in any danger, Charlotte."

"And our familiars?" I asked him. "The last time mine disappeared, he was stolen."

"Did you feel it when he was in danger?"

"Of course I did," I told him defensively.

"Do you feel that now?"

I concentrated, reaching out mentally and emotionally to the cat. After a few minutes, despite not getting an answer, I shook my head no. It was unsettling, but his lack of conversation didn't frighten me.

"We should get some sleep," Gunther said again.

"We can't just leave the circuses in the middle of Mickwac with hundreds of paranormals sleeping off a bender outside. What if some human wanders in?" I told him. He pointed up. "We can move the circus to the safe zone, but what about the cats? They won't be able to get back."

"Your parents have an animal shelter," Gunther pointed out. "Lots of stray cats coming around won't look too insane. It will look like a jailbreak. They can let us know if they show up."

"Let me call my Mom on the cauldron," I told him. "I'm just too exhausted to hike up to the house."

Now that Gunther had introduced the idea of

sleep, I could feel the exhaustion in my bones. He was right; it had been a crazy night. As much as I could operate *without* sleep, hours of being unconscious was approximately as tantalizing as the puppy stall.

~

We moved the circus, and no one was the wiser. Though a few people here and there were awake, most were fast asleep. Once we landed in the ringmaster realm, Gunther grew quiet and turned the place from morning to night to ensure those sleeping outside wouldn't get sunburned.

We fell into bed.

Before my head hit the pillow, the dreams started.

I could see my hands before me, nails short and unpolished, grasping a spoon. "Okay," I heard myself say, "here comes the airplane!"

What the heck?

I raised the spoon high above my head and made sounds as it slid down, down, down toward the mouth of a plump, cooing baby. "Now, don't spit on me like last time." The baby squealed when I shoveled green goo into its mouth, and suddenly it mirrored the sound I had just made—

in order to cover me with the food I had just
fed it.

"Rollie!" I yelped, and the baby shrieked with
laughter.

I struggled to speak, but I could not control
myself. It was disconcerting to look out of my
own eyes and feel no control over my mouth, my
body.

"How's my grandson?" Roland Makepeace
said as he strolled over to the highchair. "Gerda,"
he announced. "I think the boy's grown again!"

"Can I feed him? Can I?" little Anna begged,
jumping up and down. "I've been practicing,
watch!" Anna's face screwed up tightly with
concentration and her hand went from slightly
transparent to opaque. Slowly, steadily, she
reached out for another spoon and lifted it.

"That's very good, favorite sister-in-law," I
heard myself say.

"You're silly, Charlotte. I'm your *only* sister-in-
law," the little girl giggled.

"She's been doing wonderfully with her
lessons," I heard Gunther say from the corner of
the room. Looking up, I saw my husband staring
back at me. He was older, but not much older. His
grin was broad and his eyes warm.

"I'm so glad to hear it!" I informed him. "It

won't be too long before Rollie here will accompany you both."

"What time is everyone coming for Thanksgiving?" Gerda asked as she came out of the kitchen.

"Devana and Scout will be here with their brood on Tuesday," Gunther told his mom. She stopped next to him with her arm on his shoulder. "Tabitha and Bob think they'll be here sometime Wednesday. It all depends on traffic. Their motorhome goes a bit slower than everything else, anyway. On a holiday week?" Gunther made a pfft sound.

"Are Fiona and Ningul going to be able to make it?" I heard myself ask.

"She's close to giving birth, and Ningul doesn't want to risk the trip from Scotland," Gunther called across the room to me. "I don't think she would come, anyway. She doesn't want to risk the chance that the babe would be born in the United States."

"Yeah, that's not objectionable at all," I heard myself laugh. "Hey, I have a shift today at the animal shelter. Can you take Rollie and give him a bath?" I leaned over and caught sight of two Golden Retrievers frantically licking up whatever green goo the baby had sprayed on the floor.

"I never appreciated the dogs," Samson said from a velvet cushion on top of the fireplace.

As I peered up at him, the world froze.

"What is this?" I asked him, surprised that I was able to control my own voice now. The observed me's tone had sounded sharp and clear, but my voice (the one I seemed to be able to control) sounded far away and muffled.

"Gunther asked you what you needed," Samson said and then he yawned. "Your brain is trying to work out what you need."

"This isn't the circus," I told him as I glanced around.

Walking to the window, I stared out and caught sight of the sanctuary an acre away. My parents' house was on the other side, and the two houses and the shelter were set up in a U-shape around what looked to be a teeny, permanent fair. "Some circus stuff is out there, but there's no big top, no yurts for people to live in. How could I prefer this?"

"Why does anyone need anything?" Samson asked me.

"Are you telling me I don't want the circus? That they both get destroyed?" I asked him in a panic.

"Calm down. I'm not telling you anything,"

Samson answered haughtily. "You're working this through all on your own. I'm not even here."

I turned around and watched the cat suspiciously.

"You don't believe me?"

"Well, no one seems to know what the heck a guardian is," I said, leaning against the window. "So, it wouldn't shock me if you had a skill like this, where you could interject yourself into my dreams. I mean, you could do it in my head, so why not—"

"You're not focusing on the issue."

"And what's the issue?"

"Whether I'm definitely here? That isn't the question." Samson stood up, stretched, and bolted down. "The question is whether this is genuinely what you want. And if so, is it what you should do?"

"Do?" I laughed. "I can't *do* this. I can't even find *you*."

Samson rolled his eyes ceilingward.

"Let's say for the sake of argument that you could." Samson bounced up on the windowsill and gazed out across the expanse my imagination had conceived. "Let's say everything you just saw is achievable. Is this what you choose?"

"I don't know," I told him.

"Well, you have a limited time to grow up and decide, Charlotte." Samson exhaled sharply and surged up at me, his back legs on the sill and his paws on my chest. He peered into my eyes. "We are almost to the circus, and with every step we take your choice gets closer and closer."

"What choice?"

"Either you are *playing* dumb, or it's *not* a performance," Samson said insultingly. "Stop fighting your future, stop hiding from what you wish, stop pretending you're not equipped to be what you are. You have all you need to carry out this judgment."

"What ch—"

"If you ask me that *one more time*, I will *bite* your nose, and we will find out just how *here* I am," Samson snapped and swiped at my nose with his paw. "This is the last act of this play, and you have a starring role. Get ready."

I recognized with a start that I could feel Samson's soft paw on my nose, the press on my chest. In this dream, I had no shield. I was exposed. How could that be what I wanted?

Wait…wasn't that what I wanted? I shook my head in confusion. Everything here was hazy, unreal. Well, everything I saw was crisp. I was hazy.

And confused.

"You can finish this," Samson hissed. Then he blinked lazily, his expression relaxing. Leaning forward, the cat rubbed his cheek against my jaw, purring. "Everything will be fine if you trust yourself. You must trust the balance."

"Wait, what do you mean—" I screeched as I jerked awake in bed.

"Charlotte?" Gunther asked, sitting up with alarm next to me. I leaned into him and heard the familiar clink of our armor. I immediately shared with him the dream, what I'd seen, what Samson had expressed.

"You saw our son?" Gunther asked in a strangled sigh, tears springing to his eyes. "Oh, Charlotte," he whispered as he grasped me securely. I could almost feel him.

Almost.

CHAPTER 15

"Do you think Ms. Elkins played a trick on you?" Tabitha asked me skeptically. She bounced around the room. Kyle and Aidan, Fiona and Ningul, Scout and Devana all stared at her with shock. Bob leaned in and whispered something to her.

"Ms. Elkins would not do such a thing," Devana told Tabitha.

"Since I've been here, that woman was less than helpful in oh so many ways," Tabitha told the huntress witch. "I can't believe, though, that she's terribly gratified that Charlotte ejected her from the circus. So, you know, it's something to contemplate."

"I think Samson was real," I told Tabitha.

"Maybe everything else was my imagination, but Samson was literally in my dream."

"Do you have any proof of that?" Aidan asked.

"Does she ever have any proof of anything? And besides, aren't you allegedly able to look in someone's past?" Tabitha asked him. "Why don't you just use your skill and figure out if it was really him?"

"A dream isn't something that *happened*," Aidan explained to her. "I can't see dreams. If I could, it would be impossible for me to sift through things that took place and things that were imagined."

Tabitha shook her head. "Right. I forgot. All the rules that wrap themselves around you people and make your powers completely meaningless in critical situations. My bad."

Leave it to Tabitha to make a group of powerful paranormal beings feel like morons.

"Ms. Elkins is gone," Devana said decisively.

"Why are you so sure?" Gunther asked her.

"She told me once that Charlotte would renounce her," Devana said. I caught the huntress witch leaning in close to Scout, his arm resting casually on her back. "I didn't recall it until this morning." Frowning, she continued, "In fact, it was hidden in my mind until today. Or so it seems. Had I remembered, I would have mentioned it before now."

"She's the one that tried to kill Gunther's father?" Tabitha pointed to Devana. I nodded. "Right. Things hiding in *her* mind on purpose isn't scary at all," Tabitha pointed out with a shiver.

"I was reared by a fate-weaver, human," Devana told Tabitha defensively. "Those that spin the fates of men and paranormals sometimes call for things to be obscured from our sight for reasons known solely to them."

"Right," Tabitha said, nodding across the room at the huntress witch. "Like murder? Yeah, no, I get it, Devana. We're clear."

Devana frowned.

"Okay, first, let's not goad each other about things that happened in the past," I told everybody, staring especially at Tabitha. She rolled her eyes, but then raised her hand and nodded. "You're all here because I depend on you. Scout," I said, turning to the werebear leader. "Why have you all shown up? What is it you think will happen here?"

"Truthfully? I have no idea," Scout said with a laugh. "Our shaman told us at the last full moon that we had to travel here to witness—"

Fortuna Delphi burst through the door and hollered "Stop!"

Scout Trout stopped talking and gawked at Fortuna.

"You can't tell her," Fortuna said in a rush. Turning to the quiet Ningul, she exhorted him. "You, either."

"*What* are you talking about?" Fiona demanded.

I sighed and wondered what fresh hell this was.

"Are you going to join the group that demands people keep information from me?" I asked her, rising up and putting my hands on my hips. "Because, you know, I'm getting kind of tired of those people. Is this because I didn't let you give me a reading last night?"

"No, Charlotte, this is not some kind of retribution." Fortuna shook her head. "I'm trying to protect you—"

"I'm *also* tiring of people trying to protect me."

"I know you are, I know you are, and I wish...I don't need you to sit for a]reading," Fortuna said looking down. It was then I noticed she carried a canvas in her hand. "I need you to look at this. I need you to look at this and tell me what it is."

Fortuna held up the canvas and turned it around. On the canvas, re-created in exquisite detail, was the image of the baby from my dream. Rollie smiled, his eyes shining with the happiness only babies can project. His toothless grin seemed to reach into my soul and twist my heart into knots.

"Charlotte, that's him, isn't it?" Gunther asked me. "The baby from your dream. Our...*our* son." I nodded, unable to speak. "But...But how did Fortuna know what he looked like? What does this mean?"

"Aw, Charlotte, he's adorable," Tabitha said as if everything that was happening was normal.

"The Seer has seen one potential future," Devana told Gunther, and then she glanced up at me. "The human is right, Charlotte, your son will be delightful."

"Then it was *not* just a dream?" Ningul asked, confused.

"Wait a minute." Fiona turned toward Fortuna. "Why can *you* show her that painting of some maybe future child, but Scout can't tell her what his shaman said?"

Fortuna's eyes looked tormented. "She must

decide whether she wishes to know about the events. She must consider the impact of what you say, and should have the right to receive or not—"

"What is this garbage?" Fiona demanded. "We are paranormals, life flings prophecy at us on a near-daily basis." Fiona looked around, aggravated. "What is she *talking* about?"

I waved at Fiona to quiet her. "The decision I have to make," I responded, my eyes meeting Fortuna's across the room. "What I decide dictates whether that child becomes real, doesn't it?"

"Do you truly wish for me to answer your question?" Fortuna asked me. The room fell silent as everyone stared back and forth between the two of us. "Because it is more than that, and you know it."

She was right. It wasn't just the baby. It was the life I saw in the drea*m*. Sure, I *felt* happy, but everyone I was supposed to protect other than my immediate family was...gone.

"Why is it just my vote?" I challenged her, frustrated. "Why isn't it Gunther's decision, too?"

"He has made his choice although he does not even know the options yet consciously," Devana intoned as if she were making a proclamation with all the gravity of history. "Gunther has always been who he is, and the choice they will present him with truly is no choice. He will do what he will do because he must. Because of who he is."

Gunther's face remained impassive, but I could see the surprise in his eyes.

"So, wait, he's the steady one?" I asked, a little miffed. "No one knows what I'm going to do because who I am isn't quite set yet? Is that what you're saying?"

"Do you *really* need someone else to answer that question, Charlotte?" Tabitha asked me. I scowled at her.

"Just tell me whatever you have to tell me," I told Fortuna wearily. I sat back down on the couch feeling defeated. "I'd rather have all the info that I can."

"Before the end of this day, you will be the last ringmaster," Fortuna said, her eyes filling with tears. "Before the sun rises once more, your future will be set and you will make your choice."

My stomach churned as Gunther turned white.

"Your destiny moves with all speed toward this place, and you cannot avoid the choice," Fortuna finished. She looked down and wiped the tears from her cheeks. "I am so sorry, my friend," she whispered. "You as well," she nodded toward Gunther.

"Why are you sorry?" I asked her. "Out of the options I have, which I presume you know, aren't *any* good?"

No one responded.

CHAPTER 16

GUNTHER AND I WENT IN OPPOSITE DIRECTIONS, away from each other, after we left the yurt. We didn't even talk about it, just looked at one another, nodded, and turned away. I realized that he would go find (and sober up) Wayland Black. He understood I had to process what I heard. Alone.

"Mind if I walk with you?" Scout Trout slipped into stride beside me without waiting for approval. For I moment, I considered protesting, but his presence was oddly soothing. "A lot has happened to you since we last met."

"That's an understatement." I grinned weakly.

"Can I ask you a question?" Scout asked me

after we rounded the corner and walked slowly toward the lion yurt. I nodded. "Have you asked any of these people why they are here? Why they remain at a circus that has no established place to call home?"

"Well, no, but I was told that the purpose of the circuses was to maintain a place for folk to hide from the Witches' Council," I explained after considering the question. "Most of these people, their households, joined years ago. So, most are here because they've always been here, I presume."

"I see," Scout nodded casually as we went on walking. I didn't get the sense that he saw, actually. "Can I ask you another question?"

"Shoot."

"The circus energy was supposed to be one of building, right?" Scout stopped walking and shifted to stare down at me. Lord, the werebear leader was a massive, fierce-looking dude. His eyes, though, were friendly as he studied me. "That's what I hear—Eiggam was standing still, Maggie moving forward. At least that's how Devana tries to interpret it to me."

I nodded again. "I think it may be more intricate than that, but that's close enough."

"Well, don't you require both?"

"I guess we have both, now," I told him. "I'm full of one spirit and Gunther's full of the other."

"But solely the two of you can access it?" He crossed his arms over his chest. I nodded again. "And if you turn into the only ringmaster, does that mean one set of powers goes away? That after all this, one prevails?"

"To tell you the truth, I don't know."

"It just seems risky to me to take important powers and lock them up inside two individuals. Or one individual," Scout said, jerking his head in my direction. "You are my clan sister and so I am here, as clan leader, to stand by you if you require me."

"Well, thanks, Scout—"

"But as clan leader," he interrupted, holding a finger up, "and not as your clan brother, I cannot help but think with the Witches' Council powers in the hands of someone ethical, it is time for all of this to be given back to the people to do with what *they* will. To end the citadels and jails and controls constructed to bully us."

I frowned. "What do you mean?"

He lifted his hands and settled them on my shoulders. "You are my sister, and I care for you. I have oathed to you," Scout breathed. "But this war is done. Unless we now must bow to you and Gunther as the current King and Queen of the realm—"

I burst out laughing. "You must be joking. Gunther and me royalty? That's—"

"—fact," Scout finished seriously, and my laugh stopped abruptly. "And if Gunther is truly foretold to surrender his ringmaster powers today, then you will be the new Mina by moon's rise. And as much as I like you, Charlotte," Scout said severely, his eyes clouded with apprehensions he had not yet expressed. "I must fear you."

"I'm nothing like Mina!" I declared furiously.

"I'm sure *Mina* was nothing like Mina once," Scout pointed out.

"You think I should destroy the circuses," I told him. It sounded more like an accusation.

"I think you should think about *all* your options," Scout said, and he regarded me, his face impenetrable. "Your dream was about what *you* want deep in your core, Charlotte. We all have those dreams, too." Scout held out his hand toward the paranormals gathered under Hilde's tent. "Think about what it has felt like to have someone else in charge of your destiny."

I spun back and looked at him.

"Realize that's how we've all felt, all the time, for several generations," Scout smiled. "Maybe it's time for a change."

My dad discovered me in the puppy stall, flat on my back, buried by several litters of squirming, licking, yelping, nibbling puppies.

"Rough day?" he asked over the stall door with a smirk.

"When isn't it a rough day?" I groaned and looked back at the ceiling.

"Tabitha came up to the house and let us know what was going on," Dad told me. I raised my head up and gawked at him in confusion. Tabitha was a human being. There's no *way* she should have been able to travel down here without me. "Bob. The lares can transport people to and from the circus," Dad explained, catching my apprehension.

I settled my head back down and peered back up at the ceiling. Awesome. Something else I didn't know.

"Do you want to talk about it?" Dad asked brightly. He opened the fence and entered the enclosure. I reached up toward him and he hauled me to a vertical position. With a scoot I leaned my back against the wall, and he dropped down next to me. "We can just sit here if you like."

"No, I just…I don't know what I want."

"That's not what it sounds like to me at *all*," Dad chuckled.

"Okay, smarty-pants, what does it sound like to you?"

"It sounds to me like you know what you want." He squeezed my knee like he used to when I was a kid. "It also sounds to me like you're not sure if you're allowed to want it."

"Allowed? Dad," I gave a mournful laugh. "I'm one of the two most powerful magical beings on the planet—"

"I think the dragons are still around here and there, so you *may* be wrong about that," Dad disagreed. "But for the sake of argument, let's say you are." He paused. "What does that have to do with anything?"

"Well, there are certain agreements that come with—"

"Charlotte Astley, my father was a ringmaster, and my brother was a ringmaster. Are you honestly going to explain to me what being a ringmaster *entails*?"

"But there are obligations—"

"To who, to Maggie?" Dad asked with a snort. "She gone, and so is Eiggam. They got out of Dodge and left you holding the bag, calling a truce to the original fight. So, there's no obligation there."

"What about the people in the circus?"

"The ones that were sheltering from the Witches' Council? Do they need to do that now? I hear one of the Council is vacationing at your circus with Gerda."

"Then why haven't they left?"

"The people residing at the circus? Where would they go? The circus is their home."

"Argh!" I shouted and combed my fingers through my hair. "See, that's what I mean! Obligations!"

"Have you presented them with an option?" Dad asked me gently. "Have you told them it's safe to leave? Is Imperatorial City opened up to anyone that wants to live there now? Can paranormals safely live in the human world again?" Dad pelted me lightly with queries. "If you have any duty to them at all, Charlotte, it's revealing the war is over. Then give them their options."

"I don't even know who's in charge of the paranormal government at the moment," I confessed to him.

He chuckled so loud and so long that I started to feel a little hurt by it. "Honey, you and Gunther are the most powerful beings on the planet right now. *You* are in charge of the government. You and Gunther. If you want to be. Why else would the head of every—"

Dad paused and sat straight up. "Oh...my."

"What?" I asked him, my eyes wide.

"Oh, dear," Dad snorted, and then he drew in a deep breath. "Oh, my goodness. That's more kitty litter than I think we—"

"Dad!"

"Your cats are back."

"Samson?" I demanded, hopping up.

"Not just Samson," he answered and pushed up to stand next to me. "All of them. And they've brought someone with them."

"Who?" I asked as I followed him out. He burst into a run, and so did I. "Dad? Who's with them?"

"Mina World," he called back and lunged out the back door.

Mina had seen better days.

The cats were dozens and dozens deep in a semi-circle around a haggard, panting Mina outside of the shelter barn. Her eyes raised slowly to meet mine, and they flared with a bitter hostility. "What do you want of me?" she choked through bruised lips. Her cloak was damaged in dozens of spots as if the cats had yanked her here with their teeth.

"Me?" I asked with surprise. "I didn't want you here. Frankly, Mina, I hoped that I would never see you again."

"Then what is the purpose of this?" she shrieked. She thumped her fist against the dusty ground and swung to confront the cats. "Why have you dragged me across this barren, dreary land only to deposit me in front of my adversary! Why?"

"They want you to free them," my father informed her. The cats stared attentively at the fallen witch. "You imprisoned these men and women in these cats, and they wish their bodies and their lives back."

"They should have come to me and begged me

when I *had* the power instead of escaping to Gunther's circus," Mina scoffed. She stood up haltingly, wearily, and scraped the dirt from her black robe. "Without Eiggam's strength, I can do nothing. Their seizure of me has been nothing but a waste of time."

"It *was* fun," Samson said. He and Delilah walked forward from the cluster.

"Shut up," Mina snapped at my familiar. "Even if I had his power, I wouldn't spend it to free these miserable wretches. Freeing all these witches would exhaust me of my energy, so far and so fast that I would never get it back! I would never…"

Mina kept ranting and howling, but my head whirled and her voice faded as it all clicked into place.

Gunther would free the witches because he had Eiggam's strength, and that was who he was. He wouldn't let them stay imprisoned just so he could keep his ringmaster power. That wasn't Gunther.

If what Mina said was true, once he succeeded? Gunther would no longer be a ringmaster. Would we still be married? Would he even be a witch anymore?

Just as predicted.

Before the day ended, I would be the last ringmaster, the head of the Magical Midway and the Makepeace Circus.

Whether the two circuses remained?

That would be solely up to me.

CHAPTER 17

"GET OFF ME!" MINA SHRIEKED WHEN ONE OF THE cats leaped to her shoulder and hissed. We had moved the entire group—people, cats, prisoner—back to the cats' shed at the Makepeace Circus. After a brief surge of noses touching in what I assumed was celebration for a completed mission, all shining feline eyes lasered in on their prey.

If Mina thought her day couldn't get any worse, the cats and witches she had menaced during her term as commander of the Witches' Council did their finest to establish that was a mistaken hypothesis.

One tomcat walked up to her indifferently

and sprayed her. I stared wordlessly at the yellow liquid dripping down Mina's leg in disgust.

"Can't you stop this?" she howled at me.

"I...I, um..." The tomcat's action caught me betwixt being overwhelmed and between pointing at the karma running down the evil witch's leg while laughing. "I really don't *control* anyone, Mina. The cats have a pretty legitimate issue with you. If you'd turned them back into people, maybe you guys could have worked this out. Now?" I shrugged and nodded toward a small black cat taking a swipe at her toes.

"That one isn't even a Galenite!" she wailed. "I did nothing to that one!"

"You imprisoned her father," Dad informed her.

"Oh, well, sure," Mina huffed and rolled her eyes. "Still! She wouldn't exist if it wasn't for me!"

The young cat swiped at Mina's ankle and drew blood.

"You know, you are a witch," I told her with some irritation. "Can't you safeguard yourself somehow? Maybe levitate so they can't swipe at you?"

"Mother was never the best of witches," Devana said. She shoved the barn door open and came in, glaring at her haggard mother on the floor. "Were you, Mother?"

"No worse than that...that..." she pointed toward me and grasped for an affront that I was sure would be vulgar, but her voice trailed off as more cats moved toward her menacingly. She clambered on top of a hay bale and snatched the pitchfork that had been resting against it. Waving it toward the cats, she squealed, "I told you! I cannot undo what I have done! Leave me alone!"

"I don't think Mother learned that cats will eat their own owners when they die if they're hungry enough. Even those they loved," Devana told me, and I shuddered. "If she had, maybe she could have imagined what they'd do to those they loathe."

"I'm not dead!" Mina screamed at her estranged daughter.

"Give them a few minutes!" Devana shouted back.

"Do you really want these cats to *eat* her?" I challenged the huntress.

"You don't really want me to answer that," Devana murmured. Her eyes followed the tiny furry panthers as they circled the ever more frantic witch.

"Her influence is clearly no longer a threat,"

Scout said to Devana, his face puzzled. "Why continue to punish her?"

"You're such a compassionate soul," Devana whispered to him, nuzzling his face admiringly. "It is not for me to punish her. I helped defeat her, and it was adequate for me. You helped me see that. For them?" Devana pointed to the hundreds of angry cats, their tails flicking. "This ordeal has not yet concluded."

"It is not my fault!' Mina shouted at the cats.

At least fifty hissed back.

"I did what I had to do to keep the—"

"You did what you did to ensure that you could keep your own authority, Mother." Devana walked away from Scout and peered up at the woman who bore her. "When you had that power, you were very clear about why you were doing things."

"That is not true—"

"It is true." Mercy strode in, her voice reverberating through the room. Behind her, Roland and Gerda Makepeace clung to one another, their expressions heartbroken. Little Anna walked beside them looking flustered. "And to remedy your mistakes, even *more* will lose."

"Traitor!" Mina screamed, her eyes large.

"Yes, I misled you," Mercy nodded, walking in

with the Makepeace family. "I betrayed you when I finally understood that you didn't believe in anything other than your own power. You cared nothing for the communities you led. You killed —" Mercy's voice cracked, and her body convulsed as if someone had struck her. "You killed Gerda."

"I had to—"

"In killing her, you sowed the seeds for your *own* downfall," Mercy pronounced, cutting off the woman she once served. "It was your first mistake. Had you figured out how our world functions, you would have known that."

"What do you mean?" Mina demanded, eyeing a brilliant white cat pacing menacingly at the base of her hay bale.

"She means that what you did to them?" Gunther said as he strolled in the door, Wayland Black behind him. He stood towering, his shoulders back, and glared at Mina with sharp eyes. "I will do to *you*."

Roland Makepeace choked back a whimper.

"It has to be this way," Gunther whispered to me as he held me. "The circuses were previously joined, *you* can protect everyone if they need protection. I'm the only one that can make this right."

"I know," I confessed to him. The knot in my throat was thick, and uncomfortable. "But what about—"

"Wayland and I have spoken." He gestured toward the cyclops. Wayland's one eye glared at me accusingly, as if this was my fault. And... well...maybe it was. I shifted away from his fierce stare. "He'll help you with anything you need. Mina may be overthrown now, but the woman gave up her own child to try to capture power. She needs to be taken out once and for all."

"But maybe there's another way," I protested half-heartedly. I recognized that no matter what, Gunther would free those cat witches. If our positions were reversed, it's what I would do. It's what any respectable person would do.

"You know there isn't," Gunther smiled, reached out, and cupped my cheek. "Hey, come on, it's not like I will leave. We'll still have each other. They'll have their lives back. The risk of Mina will be over once and for all. The circus will still have a ringmaster."

"It all sounds so perfect, all tied up in a nice little ball," I mumbled back. We'd had little discussion about what, specifically, would happen to us at the end of this. It was characteristic of us, though—do what has to be done, first. Figure out what it all means second. "Will we still be married?"

"I don't know," Gunther said, tilting his head. "Didn't you regret the fact we didn't have a wedding? We could have one, you know. Just to make sure."

"You know, you haven't even *asked* me—" I started to mutter when Wayland Black shouted at me in annoyance.

"You know, some of us have *friends* locked inside those cats, princess!" the blacksmith griped at me. "Do we need to wait for him to run and get a ring, or can we *get on with this already?*"

"I didn't realize your ears were as big as your eye!" I snapped at him, blushing furiously. I wanted to argue with him, but he was right. These witches had waited long enough, and no matter what waited for Gunther and me at the other end of this, we needed to move forward and face it.

"Are you ready?" Gunther asked me as he leaned in to kiss me.

No.

I responded yes.

The love of my life turned and faced Mina World.

And then he gave up everything that had bound us together.

~

It was almost anti-climactic.

Gunther closed his eyes, raised his hands, and a dense fog filled the barn. As the pink mist floated its way through the enclosed area, tiny gray cubes of galena sprung up to hover in the air. Suspended for mere seconds, they fired across the expanse to smash into the erstwhile head of the Witches' Council.

In the end, there were approximately a thousand witches, nude, standing in the barn.

One witch, fully dressed, bowed before them in exhaustion.

"Gunther," I called out, but Wayland Black clasped my arm in a vise grip and held me back. "What are you doing!" I shouted at him. I spun, glowering at his hand on my arm. "Let go of me!"

"*Calm* yourself, sweetheart," he sighed. "Gunther has no armor anymore. If you go over there all bothered and overwrought, you could snatch him too rough and kill him. Just *calm* yourself, Ringmaster. That's all I'm saying."

I held up, watching.

Gunther's family floated over to check on him. He peered up at his father, his face coated with perspiration. His eyes were anguished. "Dad, I'm sorry," he whispered. "It had to be done, but I'm so sorry. I feel like I failed you."

"Sorry?" Roland said, his voices filled with affection. "Son, you just saved hundreds of our kind. I'm so proud of you, Gunther. Your mother and I both are," he declared. He looked up, his eyes found me, and we nodded to one another. My powers, my own powers, washed over me like a wave. I could discern that he meant what he said to his son.

But it also devastated him.

The Makepeace Circus was no more, and his family's long history and legacy was over.

"Gotcha!" Devana shouted as she scruffed the last Galenite cat. The silver mark glowed on its backside as the black cat flailed in all directions with extended claws. A grumbling screech emanated from Mina as she struggled like a rabid boxer against the air. "Well, I guess scruffing doesn't quiet her down."

"It will," a naked brown-haired woman spoke

to the huntress witch. She cradled a tomcat against her chest. "The longer we are within the cat, the more cat and witch become one."

I looked around and abruptly realized there were a lot fewer cats in the outbuilding. "I thought she held you all *in* the cats. Wouldn't Gunther have split the two of you?" I asked her as I craned my neck around the barn. "I see a lot of witches, but not a lot of cats. Are they okay?"

"They are us, and we are fine," the woman answered, and I noticed a layered cadence to her tone. "We have been one, and so we are one."

"Oh, wow…" Devana said, her eyes opening wide.

I still didn't understand. "What am I missing?"

"We are still Galenite cats, your greatness," the woman told me and bowed. The cat in her arms bowed its head toward me as well. "We are simply no longer held by force to one form."

With a whisper, the naked woman shrank down and grew into a cat again. A few moments later, she returned to her humanoid form.

"My mother accidentally invented a new race of witches," Devana said, awestruck. "And Gunther set them free."

"Can we even *do* that?"

"Maybe not *you,*" Roland Makepeace told me

haughtily as he sauntered over. "My son, on the other hand, can do anything he sets his mind to."

"Roland, *stop* that," Gerda admonished him. "Charlotte, Roland is only teasing you. It was simply a side effect of that *foolish* woman's evil," she said. She scowled at the prizefighting cat in Devana's hand. "I doubt *she* thought about what she was doing. But when her curse met the love Gunther had for them, the sacrifice he made for them?"

"Love always conquers evil in the end," Devana told me.

I glanced over at the weary-looking Gunther. Naked witches threw themselves into his arms and thanked him. I realized I should *probably* be jealous or concerned or alarmed or something, but it didn't seem any weirder than anything else that'd been happening lately.

"What are you going to do with your...um... mother?" I asked Devana.

"Torture her," Devana deadpanned as she shook the cat lightly. The cat froze and eyed Devana warily.

"Dee," Scout said, his look faintly pained.

"Oh, calm *down*," Devana told him and rolled her eyes. "I'm not going to *torture* her. I doubt there's much more I could do. The humiliation alone must be driving her slightly mad. I am, though," she said as she lifted the cat and looked into its eyes, "going to attempt to teach this creature right from wrong."

The cat cringed, and then hissed.

"Oh, do be quiet, Mother," Devana told her, and then laughed. "This is going to be far more fun than it should be."

It took several hours for all the witches to say their thanks to Gunther, and despite his exhaustion, he stayed until the last one had enveloped him in a naked hug.

"You know, you have superpowers," Tabitha said when she walked in, Bob trailing behind her as always. "You could have put clothing on all of them with a snap of your fingers before they pressed their bosoms against your husband."

I didn't respond, but I kicked myself for not thinking of that.

"The Magical Midway is expanding again," Tabitha mumbled. "Bob and I wanted to let you know. It's like the two circuses are…I don't know, they're…"

"Morphing into one?" I guessed.

"Yeah, I guess."

"That's because I'm the only ringmaster left," I told her as I watched Gunther walk slowly toward us. "One ringmaster. One circus."

"So, wait—are you and Gunther still married?"

Silence.

"Charlotte?" Tabitha pressed.

"Look, I don't *know*, okay? How much of this is magic, a choice, destiny, an oath, a prophecy," I told her angrily, "I don't know. Are you okay?" I asked Gunther as he reached us. I clutched my arms so as not to grab him, Wayland's warning echoing in my head.

"I don't feel much different, actually," he said wearily. "You?"

I shook my head no. "Maybe..."

Gunther shook his head. "I tried to teleport over here, just to see. No dice," he told me, smiling sadly. "I'm definitely out of ringmaster powers."

I looked down.

"All hail Queen Charlotte," Tabitha joked.

I raised my eyes. Gunther and I stared at one another in silence.

CHAPTER 18

"WELL, NOW YOU'VE DONE IT!" MS. ELKINS trudged through the crowd of Magical Midway folks, Makepeace Circus folks, and naked Galenite witches. "Get some clothes on these people, Charlotte! They're clad in nothing but the sky!"

"I thought I *exiled* you?" I asked her.

"You banished me from the *Magical Midway*, but this isn't that Magical Midway, *is* it? Now it's the *Makepeace Magical Midway Morphing circus featuring naked cat-witches!*" Ms. Elkins harrumphed and wildly flailed her cane through the air.

"I swear, the technicalities that govern this place? They give me a sense of ceaseless wonder,"

Tabitha whispered, leaning into me. Bob tugged her away from me and shook his head *no*, pointing strongly toward Ms. Elkins and furiously whispering.

"Why are you here?" I sighed as I flattened my shirt down.

"First, to help these poor children get clothing, clearly!"

I snapped my fingers, imagined cloaks on all the naked people, snapped again. Within the blink of an eye, the cat-witches were clothed. "Happy now?"

A chorus of protests erupted from the direction of the bathhouse.

Oops.

We had only been standing in the open for a few moments, but the anxiety of those around us fluttered into my perception. It felt kind of like water being let into a confined area. First, it was splashing around my ankles, but once the force of it struck my knees, I started to get worried.

I pulled my eyes away from the norn and looked around.

Gunther's people were staring carefully at me, flanked by Tabitha on one side and Wayland on the other. My own people were staring at Gunther's people, and the clans that had showed up to witness…something…watched everyone quietly.

"Let's go to my yurt," I told Ms. Elkins. "We're not doing this here."

"What are you hiding?" someone shouted indignantly.

"That whatever she will say will probably freak you out," I called back to the heckler while pointing at Ms. Elkins. "She freaks me out constantly, and I'd like to spare you the concern. It will be unnecessary, to boot, because I doubtless won't do what she wants me to, anyway."

There was a long pause and low murmurs from the crowd.

"Okay, that's fair!" the same voice yelled back sounding less annoyed.

"Thanks for your understanding! Ms. Elkins?" I said. "My yurt, please? And could the clan leaders of whatever clans are here join us?"

The crowd murmured its surprise.

"This is ridiculous," Ms. Elkins protested. "I need to speak to you alone."

"You can speak to me alone," I told her, smiling. "This is a circus, though, Ms. Elkins. Don't you realize by now that everyone knows everyone else's business? I'm just getting ahead of the delay, that's all."

She looked like she wanted to argue, but all eyes were on her, and she felt it. They watched and waited, nervously, to see what the norn would do.

Without responding, she turned and began waddling toward the dormitory yurt that had been the scene of so many decisive moments, so many compromises that seemed insignificant.

As we followed, all seemed to feel the significance this time.

"How could you let him sacrifice his circus for those misbehaving cats?" Ms. Elkins started as soon as we crossed into the room. "Didn't any of you think to check with anyone about the prophecy? What happens when there is only one ringmaster left?" she asked me.

Scout Trout took up a position on the side of the room, and many other clan leaders followed his lead. Surrounding us on the periphery, they watched the two of us as we stood across from one another. Their faces shone concern, their eyes bouncing back and forth between us.

"Okay, Ms. Elkins. What happens when there is only one ringmaster left?" I asked her.

"Destruction!" she snapped at me with a piercing look. "You, girl, have lost your two gods, your husband, you got rid of your fate-weaver. Your past reader has been less than useless." She cast a skeptical glance at Aidan with her back stiff, her face set in a grimace. "You have nothing left but yourself now!"

I looked at her for a moment, and then I began to laugh.

"What's so funny?" she asked me, her eyes narrowing.

I kept laughing. Gunther looked at me with concern.

"I demand that you answer me!" Ms. Elkins said, looking offended.

I laughed harder.

"Charlotte, I know that she can be a bit of a pain," Roland said, floating next to me. "But I'm not sure that your amusement is getting us anywhere."

Tabitha chuckled.

"Oh, don't *you* start, human," Roland grumbled.

"I'm sorry, I'm sorry," I said. My laughter

slowed. Wiping the tears from my eyes, I turned to Roland. "It's just that I just figured it out."

"Oh?"

"Figured what out, Charlotte?" Gunther asked me.

"Every single time something that's been ordering me around leaves, something else pops up to take its place. Now, it's *just* me," I told Gunther. "But it's all just bull."

"We have nothing to do with this!" Farly Dillinger hollered from the corner, his dark face turning red. "The Bull Clan has not tried to give the ringmaster offense!"

"Um, no, no, I don't mean bull as in bulls," I vigorously shook my head. "I mean bull as in... um..." I looked around in confusion.

"Unicorn turds, Farly," Gunther told the bull shifter. The huge man's face relaxed and he nodded.

"What I mean is the circuses, each one of them, had this power that had very few rules," I explained, raising my voice so the crowd assembled could hear. "At least, they had few rules until our ancestors began piling them on. At my circus? I have to be on the grounds when the sun goes up or down. If not, I'm locked out until the sun rises or falls again. Why? *Why* would that be a rule?"

"It's not for you to question—"

"Hey, whoa, there, Grandma," Tabitha said with a chuckle, cutting off Ms. Elkins. "Why don't you wait and see where she's going with this?"

"Because she serves—"

"We serve who we *choose*," Devana said and. pushed herself off the wall. Turning, she handed the Mina-cat to Scout (who looked less than thrilled) and then shifted back to stare at the old woman that raised her. "You know nothing but the fate of the predestined, honored one. But not all of us wish to be ruled by fate."

"Devana," Ms. Elkins gasped, shocked. "Your life is fated—"

"I am fated to be alone. The rules of my people."

"Well, yes, but I'll always be with—"

"I do not *wish* to be alone," the huntress witch told the old woman softly, casting a glance back at Scout.

"The huntress witches take no husbands!" Ms. Elkins exclaimed, her watery eyes blinking rapidly behind her glasses. "They hunt, they mate, they birth—"

"And they are alone," Devana finished. "I do not wish to be alone."

"Devana, darling—"

"I *will not* be alone."

The room fell silent.

It startled me, the demand in Devana's voice. In one day, the huntress witch had taken on the two women who had mothered her, the two women who had decreed she would live her life alone in service to their desires, demands or mistakes.

"Well," Ms. Elkins grumbled. She gazed nervously at the witch she thought of as a daughter. "I suppose *one* huntress witch living with a man won't bring the whole system down. After all, they rejected you because of what your mother had done. We'll find you a nice witch to settle—"

"No," Devana thundered. "I love the bear clan leader."

"Hey there, ho there, now wait a minute," Bob broke in, shrugging loose of Tabitha's hand (much to her surprise). "Like, we can't have the species crossing and stuff, right? There are *rules*, yo."

"You have been attached like glue to the side of the human since she arrived, lares," Devana said with amusement as she gestured to Tabitha.

"Well, yeah, but I haven't, like, *married* her or…um…*anything*," the Roman said with a blush. Bob turned and smiled at Tabitha brightly, but her eyes were dark as she stared at the lares. His eyes blinked twice, confused. Then his smiled faded.

"Honey?" he asked gently.

Tabitha glared at him with such ferocity that his blush burned even hotter.

"Yeah, so, um, ignore me." Bob stepped back and grabbed Tabitha's hand. "We're all good now," he said, smiling cheerfully. "Right?"

Her glare continued.

Bob swallowed loudly.

"Look, I don't know *what* the rules should be," I told Ms. Elkins, and she smiled triumphantly. "Not so fast," I tilted my head. "What I *do* know is that Mina doesn't make them anymore. I do."

Out of the corner of my eye, I saw Scout's face grow tense.

"And I shouldn't. No *one* person should, just because they have more power than everyone else. And clearly things can be changed. Gunther did it with his circus," I told Ms. Elkins. "Mina did it when she took over, even though what she did was wrong."

"What are you saying?" Gunther asked me.

"I'm saying I shouldn't decide alone for everyone else."

"Then who decides?" Devana asked.

"We do. All of us."

"A vote?" Scout asked.

"Why not?" I asked him. Many of the clan leaders looked confused. Some looked frightened. Scout looked pleased, and he gave me a half smile. "First, though, I need to talk to the Magical Midway folks."

"What for?" Gunther asked.

"We're essentially a clan, the same as they are," I explained as everyone began talking amongst themselves. "But everyone is a member of another clan, too. So, we need to see what people want to do."

"So, that's the situation in a nutshell," I finished.

"That's a pretty big nut," Anya shouted.

"I'm happy to keep the circus together if there's enough interest, but it will no longer move. It will stay in Mickwac attached to the animal shelter, and because it will be noticeable, folks will have to be super careful about shifting and the like," I finished.

"What about the rules regarding human and paranormal interaction?" someone shouted.

"None of the clan leaders have ever been happy about those rules," I explained. "I doubt the death penalty for exposing who we are to humans will survive the day."

"I could go home?" one leprechaun whispered loudly.

"We could move to the plains of Africa?" Mark asked as Serena teared up. I nodded.

"You and I could go to *Scotland*, Nin," Fiona said to Ningul, her eyes shining.

"Wait a minute, wait a minute, wait a minute," Anya called out as she stepped up to the front, her fierce expression suspicious. "Our families have been working this place so long that we have nothing. Like, nothing. For those of us *without* magic, will we get some kind of help from the witches? Maybe a pot of gold from the leprechauns?"

"Yeah, we're penniless!" the elephant herd cried out.

"Hold on, hold on, hold on," I said, holding my hand up. Turning to Wayland, I waved him over and whispered to him.

"The circuses just combined, so I don't know what our resources are yet, but we have a little money saved up over the years. The Magical Midway has a couple of hundred thousand dollars we could split up," I told the crowd, quickly calculating in my head how far that would go when split among about 2500 people.

Eighty dollars each? Is that right?

"That won't even buy me a bus ticket!" someone shouted and I grew nervous about the fate of my family's shelter. Wayland slid next to me and opened a book, pointing to the number at the bottom.

"Are you serious? Is that right?" I whispered to him, shocked. He nodded. The crowd began shouting at me angrily. I looked at Gunther.

"My family invested well," Gunther told me, smiling sheepishly.

"You're rich?" I choked out.

"Well, yes, but you're powerful, so we're balanced," Gunther smiled. He looked up warily as the crowd began angrily surging toward the stage. "You better let them know. You can defend yourself, but I'm a little vulnerable here."

"Excuse me," I said standing up and shouting over the din. "Excuse me! Come on, folks! Settle down!"

"We will starve!"

"We'll have no home! What will we do?"

"How will we survive on eighty dollars! We're doomed! Doomed!"

"Gunther's circus has seventeen billion dollars, you ninnies, so no! You will *not* starve. *No one will starve*! Sheesh!"

Silence descended.

A throat cleared.

"That's..."

"Six million dollars each..."

"I'm a millionaire..." someone whispered.

"There's seven of *us*, so we're even more millionaire-ish than you!"

"Vegas, baby!" someone whooped.

Several more people echoed "Vegas! Vegas!"

"I never said it would be split equally, I'm just saying that if you go, we can help you..." I shouted, but it was futile. Half of the attendees had fled to pack, the other half were euphoric, dancing like lunatics as if they had just won the lottery.

"How do they even know the value of money, anyway?' I grumbled. I sat down sullenly. I had to admit, I was kind of hurt. My family and Gunther's family had protected these people generation after generation, and it was clear that now there was no threat but there was a windfall, everyone was ready to set off.

"They worked in the human world, they know what money is. They just never needed it," Gunther told me. "This is a good thing, Charlotte."

"Is it?"

"It's their choice," he smiled as he watched the children beg their parents for a trip to Disneyland. "It is a choice made not because of fear, but of desire. That, I think, is a good thing."

"I thought this would be harder."

"This? *This* wasn't the hard part."

"Thanks to you and your billions, Richie Rich."

Gunther smiled and pointed over toward Scout.

The bear clan leader was arguing with several other leaders, and the debate looked like it was close to coming to blows.

"That? That will be the hard part."

CHAPTER 19

"I REALIZED WHEN SHE SAID THAT," I TOLD
Gunther. I threw my old clothes in a pile and
pulled on a pair of jeans. "Ever since I became
ringmaster I've depended on everyone else. Ms.
Elkins told me what to do, or my father, or Uncle
Phil, or Samson."

"Okay, I get that part," Gunther said, politely
facing the wall of my bedroom.

"I didn't have to do it anymore. I mean…no,
not that. I never did. I *never* had to listen to any of
them when they told me what to do and what not
to do," I explained. I pulled my shirt down and
gave it a tug. "You can turn around now."

Gunther turned.

"The lesson of all of this wound up being

simple." I walked over to my make-up chair. "I'm a grown-up and I can do what I want to. I can change anything. And maybe I should."

"Charlotte, love, forgive me for saying this, but that sounds a little like megalomania."

"Does not." I frowned as I put on blush. "I didn't say I will change everything and I will make everyone feed me thousand dollar grapes while I rest on a velvet cushion being massaged by werebears," I told him, though I had to admit I had that in my pocket a little too fast to have not thought about it once or twice.

"What will you change it to?"

"That's just it," I told him as I grabbed some lipstick. "I don't think it should be my decision. But it kind of has to be something I do because I'm the only one that can. Which sucks."

Gunther sat down on the bed, his eyes troubled. After a while, I realized he was far more silent than he usually was. Turning, I studied him. "What's wrong?"

"Nothing."

My eyes narrowed. "Gunther—"

"I lost my family's circus," he said. His eyes dropped and he shifted on the bed as if his body had become slightly uncomfortable. "My father said he understood, but he hasn't spoken to me since. Even Delilah's ignoring me."

I squinted and realized for the first time since we'd met, Gunther had an air of hopelessness about him. His expressive, sensitive face was sad. I dropped my makeup and walked over to him slowly, kneeling in front of him and lightly, lightly resting my hands on his thighs.

"This has all raced forward so fast that I didn't even stop to ask you how you were feeling," I told him. "I'm so sorry, Gunther."

"This was the first major decision I made since we were together that you and I didn't talk through first." He raised his eyes and stared into mine. "I thought about it. Talking to you first, I mean. I did. But Fortuna had said what she said, and I dismissed that as being enough for you to know what I would do."

"Gunther, how could you have let those people stay imprisoned? I knew, without a doubt, the decision you would make."

"But is it the decision *we* would make?" he asked me, his eyes pained. "Did my action force you into this?"

That brought me up short. "Force me into what?"

"You're destroying your circus, now, too,"

Gunther explained, his eyes locked on mine. Thin drops of nervous perspiration had broken on out his upper lip, a lip that continued to frown. "Would you have even considered this if I hadn't done what I did? Would we be going down this path if we had talked about it?"

"First, it's not my circus, it's our *two* circuses," I corrected him. I expected a half-smile, maybe an eye twinkle, but Gunther remained dark and brooding. "Second, didn't you hear anything I've said the last few hours? I'm not doing anything because of anyone. Least of all you."

"Ouch," Gunther said with a half-smile.

"Finally, a smile," I smiled widely. "I thought we broke your face."

He chuckled, and I breathed easier.

"Look, Gunther, I came in here believing in everything I was raised with, the values my parents instilled in me." I sat down next to him on the bed and gently grabbed his hand. "For a while, I'll admit, I felt like a ping-pong ball being whacked around by the fates or powers or whatever you want to call it. I never believed in dictatorships."

"But that's our world," Gunther shrugged.

"And if I have any ability to change it, it won't be. If I want to force anyone into anything, it's just that I want people to find their own place in this world."

There was a moment of silence, and neither Gunther nor I seemed to feel the need to fill it. We gazed at one another, the history of two worlds, two people, between. Finally, he nodded.

"Say you do. What then?" Gunther asked. "You still have the powers of a god, and everyone knows it. Even if you dictate freedom, you are *still* a dictator."

"But a *benevolent* one," I joked and smiled. "So I'm still a step up from Mina."

Gunther raised his eyebrow.

"Yeah, I know," I sighed. "I haven't figured it out, either. I mean, you could spend all your power, so maybe I can spend all mine?"

"He didn't *spend* his power," Samson said. We had gathered in the main yurt to discuss the issue. "He transferred it to the witch-cats. As cats are connected to the spirit of the earth, he essentially set the power free within the feline population. Cats are all connected, they will take the power far and wide."

Tabitha and I looked at one another.

"That's not what I see," Aidan said, frowning.

"Oh, you see *nothing*," Samson told him and yawned. "Not since she banished the norn from the circus. We're outside the threads she wove, so your powers?" The cat made an odd sound. "The norn giveth and the norn taketh away."

"I'm not paranormal anymore?" Aidan asked, surprised.

"You have some residual energy about you." Samson swirled his paw in a circle toward Aidan. "If you wanted to open up a psychic detective agency to find missing people, you could probably do that." He yawned again. "But no, you can't unpack someone's life in minute detail, no. You're not needed anymore."

"Well, *that's* a little harsh, don't you think?" Kyle snapped at the cat. He put his arm around his crestfallen boyfriend.

"It's entropy," Cama, the death bat, squeaked from the rafters. "Everything is falling apart and it will keep falling apart until someone puts it all back together again."

"What do you mean *someone*?" Gunther asked.

"I mean just what I said, blue eyes," Cama told him. "Mom can explain it much better than I can. Do you guys want me to call—"

"No!" echoed the various people simultaneously.

"You've been locked in an unchanging stasis for hundreds of years," Cama said as she flew down. "Everything has to change."

"If Gunther set his power free, that means static unchanging whatever was just loosed on the world, but the creative, progressive whatever is still locked inside of me, doesn't it?" I asked the bat.

"It wasn't *loosed* on the world," Samson huffed. "The cats have it. They'll get it all where it needs to go."

"Cats control the world now?" Kyle asked.

"What do you mean *now*?" Samson leveled a look at Kyle.

"Okay, so should I give my power to dogs, then?" I joked to the group.

Samson looked scandalized.

"Water," Fortuna said as she walked in, Samantha Goodfellow behind her. "You should give your power to the water."

"The planet never gets water added to it," Fortuna explained as she sat down. "It also never *disappears* from it. It's a component of all living cells, all animals, all plants. The magic would permeate the earth and *every* living thing on it, eventually. You would, over time, give magic back to the world, Charlotte."

"Over time, the cats would take in Maggie's magic from the water, and Eiggam's magic would be displaced until they were both joined again evenly," Samson said, thinking intently. "That's actually not a bad plan."

"No one could ever take all the magic out and use it the way Mina did to subjugate you," Samantha Goodfellow explained. "It would simply be too diffused."

"How would the cats put Eiggam's magic into the water?" Kyle asked.

"You do know urine has quite a bit of water in it, no?" Samson asked haughtily.

"Ew," Kyle mumbled.

"I pee magic?" Bob asked, looking bewildered. Tabitha covered her mouth with her hand so he couldn't see her laugh at his statement.

"Okay, look, say this *would* work," I told Fortuna. "How do I get my magic *into* the water?"

"Without causing a tsunami or something?" she asked, shrugging. "That, I don't know."

"Um…maybe I can help with that?" Tabitha

said, leaning forward. We all turned to look at her.

"You still have a wish left," Fortuna gasped.

Tabitha nodded.

"Would that work?" Fortuna asked, looking at Samantha Goodfellow. The chubby priestess shrugged. The priestess looked at the magic cat, and soon all eyes turned to Samson. We waited.

"It would work, if she phrased it carefully," Samson said.

Silence descended on the group and we all looked at one another. Everyone seemed to wait for someone else to say something, to agree, to propose that we go try it out. But no one did.

Not even Samson.

"Would you be willing to do that?" I asked Tabitha after a few minutes. "It's *your* wish, and it's your last one."

"It is," she nodded. "And I would."

"Why?" Gunther asked, seemingly without thinking.

"Why not?" Tabitha asked, She leaned back again and smiled at him. "Honestly, I kind of *like* the fact that a human being keeps saving the paranormal world's butt. Besides," she said, reaching out for Bob's hand, "I have a vested interest in this circus not needing a security force anymore. Anything I can do to move that along I'm happy to do."

"Wow," Bob drawled as he stared at her. "It's almost like you're using your last wish for me." His eyes shone in his awestruck face.

"I also want my best friend back in town." Tabitha turned and smiled at me.

"Well, *that* takes some shine off that," Bob grumbled as Tabitha laughed.

CHAPTER 20

"WE DIDN'T *HAVE* A PARANORMAL GOVERNMENT," Patches Timbo, the head were-elephant at the Magical Midway, said, leaning back. The chair groaned and whined under his substantial circumference. "And no disrespect meant to you, Charlotte, but the Witches' Council didn't come to be because all of us conveyed some wish to be dominated by witches."

The assembled leaders murmured in agreement.

"We have our *own* communities, our own customs," Aldo Forest, one of the werebears, said nodding. "None of us cared much for the vagaries, persecution, and egocentricity that seemed to suffuse the Council. No offense," he said to me with a half smile. Glancing back at Mercy, he frowned and pointed. "*You* can take offense, though."

"What is she even *doing* here?" Rhodia, a werewolf, rumbled.

"There's an administration already in place, and Mercy understands that bureaucracy better than the rest of us. She helped run it," Gunther told the werewolf quietly. "Now, whether we change it, keep it, or demolish it, we need someone that knows it."

"*Keep* it? Did your little magic show with the cats *fry your brains*, lad?" Krog, the goblin, howled across the table.

Everyone began hollering at once.

"Everyone, please! Settle down," I yelled. "*No* one will impose a result here. We're gathered to talk this through and come to a solution that supports everyone going forward, not to argue with each other over things that have previously been done."

"Charlotte," Selena said sharply, studying me with golden eyes. "The things that have been done to my people were dreadful. The werelions will demand vengeance."

"As will we," Bart Billingsworth said in his nasal tone. "Her people may have been rounded up, but my people were *eaten*!" the wereduck announced, anguished. His wife, Bonnie, dabbed her eyes.

"Ducks are some good eatin'" Luca, a satyr, murmured.

"How dare you!" Bonnie exclaimed fiercely.

"People! People!" I exclaimed. Recriminations flew across the room. Interspersed among the roars were murmured comments regarding which were-animals tasted great with garlic.

"This is spiraling out of control," Gunther whispered, leaning in to me.

"My gosh, you people are worse than children!" Tabitha shouted. All heads jerked to gawk at my friend with expressions of horror. "The human world already has a bunch of rules. Why reinvent the wheel? Just follow *those* rules. No stealing. No killing. I mean, why are you guys making this so complicated?"

"Because there are far more difficulties for magical creatures than the human world can even address, young lady," Patches Timbo told her kindly. "I recognize a human won't understand—"

"This human is the only thing that's able to get rid of your superpowered dictator witch over there," Tabitha cut him off and pointed to me. "You guys really think way too much of yourselves. For goodness' sake, you're not *that* special."

There were so many gasps I couldn't even mark who gasped them.

"Now, see here, young woman," Serena started, but Tabitha held up her hand. Serena's eyes narrowed, but Mark reached out and laid a calming hand on her arm.

"You each have powers. Okay, true. *Most* of you are animal and human, you can move back and forth between them. Admittedly, super cool —but that's *one* skill," Tabitha explained. "*One* thing you can do that no one else can."

"*We* can be both at the same time," Kyle told her, crossing his arms.

"Okay, yes, sure—but again, that's *one* special skill. Humans have skills, too. Some can run fast, or create great works of art, or do stage magic or invent things. From what I can tell, you guys can shapeshift—and not much more than that."

"*I* can create gold," the leprechaun shouted.

"Can you shapeshift?" Tabitha countered.

"Well," the leprechaun paused, hesitating. "No."

"There you go, one skill," Tabitha replied. "You need one rule about your one skill. Everything else? The human world already has rules. Just use *them*."

"We *already* have rules for our clans," Anya pointed out. Many people nodded. "They have worked fine for thousands of generations."

"Well, there you go. All done, then."

The gathered group looked flustered by Tabitha's take on the simplicity of paranormal life. Scout Trout, the werebear leader, cleared his throat and leaned forward.

"Okay, say you're right. The witches *don't* have one skill," Scout Trout said as he shifted restlessly.

"Sure they do," Fortuna said as she strode forward. "Their one skill is magic.

I wasn't wholly sure I concurred with Tabitha's premise.

But for the life of me, as I looked around the room, I couldn't spot anyone whose powers were *particularly* varied. Those that could shapeshift could do little else. The leprechauns made gold. The lares could sense enemies and fight. The salamanders controlled fire. The brownies? Housework and chores. Naiads? Water. The genies—

A ha.

"Not all of us are single faceted," I told Tabitha. "What about Jeannie?"

"She grants wishes." Tabitha held up a single finger. "One skill."

"But within that one skill, there's limitless power—"

"And *also* many rules," Jeannie called from the back. "We police our own, Charlotte. There is a reason that humans have not been incinerated by a sustained djinn thought, over the years." She raised an eyebrow. "And believe me, there have been moments in your history that we spoke seriously about it."

I gulped.

"Okay, what about Cama, or her mother?" I asked.

"Are you mortal?" Tabitha looked up to the rafter and asked the bat.

"Oh, gosh, no," Cama squeaked.

"Not mortal, not of this earth," Tabitha shrugged. "We can try to make rules for the ghosts or gods or guardian spirits, but I assume that's kinda futile."

"But *I'm* not mortal, either," Bob declared, his face crestfallen.

"Look, I'm *not* saying that anything we establish here or any one set of rules will control everything," Tabitha explained. She reached out and squeezed Bob's hand. "The world has a certain amount of lawless chaos in it, even with good government—maybe it's to keep it on its toes. Maybe you immortals are crucial in ways we don't understand."

"When did this become a *we* thing?" Keith MacBlane, one of the chiefs of the kelpies, muttered, gesturing toward Tabitha.

"When you needed *my* help to unfurl this master plan that all of you *can't* agree on—and when some of you started complaining you wanted to live in the human world. If you want to be able to go in and out of the human world, you have to understand it," Tabitha shot back. "You may like it, and you may not like it, but you need humans, and they've progressed farther than you. Well, some of them. That's clear."

Keith stared back at her, his dark eyes saddened.

"I appreciated this would be a pain," I told Gunther after we called a break so folks could walk around and clear their heads. "But I didn't think it would be quite as convoluted as it is."

"It's not convoluted," Tabitha said, coming up to us, Bob trailing behind her. "You all are trying to make it complicated, but it's not."

"I agree with Tabitha," Fortuna said when she reached us, Samantha Goodfellow in tow. "The magical practices and moralities that the Priestess has been teaching me *are* simple. And yet they far exceed what anyone has ever showed me in the paranormal world, Charlotte."

"Ouch," Gunther replied, flinching.

"No, no, it's not…You taught me how to use the talents I have," Fortuna told Gunther. She placed a hand on his arm. "The Priestess has been helping me examine *whether* I should employ those talents, when I should use them, and what I need to reflect on before I use my skill to disregard someone else's will."

Gunther frowned. "They never taught us anything like that at the Academy."

"It seems to me the Witches' Council enforced their own selfish view of what witches should be," Samantha Goodfellow said quietly. "Learn your power, use it haphazardly, sow chaos. A chaotic, disorganized world has a hard time overthrowing tyrants."

"What you did was a perfect example," Tabitha said.

Gunther looked surprised. "Me?"

"When you healed Melissa Hayden." Tabitha nodded. "You didn't ask her if she wanted it, she had no explanation for it, and it sent her down a dark and destructive path."

"I'm sure you did it with the best of intentions," Samantha Goodfellow told Gunther, smiling tenderly at him. "It started, though, with an assault on her will. Had you asked me before you did it, I would have counseled against it—because she could not consent."

"And that's the core," Tabitha nodded excitedly. "Consent. Most humans live in a world where magic doesn't exist, where powers like the ones in this yurt are not truth. If you just treat all those powers, even the ones that don't act on others, as something that others must consent to experiencing—"

"And couple that with following the rules of the society in which you live," Samantha Goodfellow nodded. "Elegant, and simple. It's not about hiding who you are. It's about living in a way that only impacts others for good."

"And what if we choose to be our best supernatural selves?" Anya asked, shoving in to the group.

"You have Imperatorial City," Tabitha said,

shrugging. "Elect a mayor, elect a city council, and form a city government. People can move there if they want, but it doesn't rule everyone."

"I *hate* that name," I shuddered.

"Elysia," Mercy said. She lingered on the edge of the group. We all shifted to look at her.

"What's that?" I asked.

"Its original name was Elysia. Before Mina changed it."

"Wait…I think I have heard of the lore of Elysia," Priestess Goodfellow said, her eyes taking on a distant look.

"Likely so. Humans, if they pursued the truth of paranormals, or needed healing, could find it—if their desire, belief, or need was true."

"What about the surrounding protections?" Gunther asked. "The…the lights that glowed from half-witches, the magical lock on the barriers so no one could pass through without a Witches' Council invitation?"

"I suspect that now Mina is a cat, humans can once again find it if they have need of it." Mercy peered at the unhappy feline in Devana's arms on the other side of the room. "Her magic was likely undone with her. I'm almost sure of it."

"That would make sense," I told Gunther.

"There you go," Tabitha said. "Folks that want

to live there can live there and let their magic freak flag fly, folks that want to live in the world live in the world. Do nothing to someone else without their consent. See?" She held up her hands. "Simple!"

I sat down with a smile as everyone regathered. Gunther quietly explained what our small group had come up with.

"And who would run this new promised land, you?" Anya asked. I shook my head no. She stared at me oddly and then held up her hands. "Who would run it, then?"

"You'd have an election," Tabitha called out. "People would indicate that they wanted to be the Mayor, tell people why. Everyone in the city would vote, and you'd decide on term limits so no one person could amass too much power. There's lots of models for city government you can follow. Goal is to get the consent of the governed, and that's pretty easily done as long as you ask people."

"Until then, there will be chaos!" Kelly Brus, Fiona's sister, shouted out. Fiona sat quietly next to her, watching.

"Then you all can elect an interim Mayor," Tabitha said firmly. "The highest ranking member of each clan that wants to live in Elysia can make up the city council. You guys can all begin making a city that's more welcoming to all species, and those humans that find their way to you."

"I feel like we're being dictated to by this human," Keith deadpanned.

"This human took multiple years of political science in college, so this human has some educated suggestions, that's all," Tabitha shot back. "Have you?"

"What is political science?" Keith asked, perplexed.

"It's the study of theory and practice of government and politics at the local, state, national, and global levels," Tabitha rattled off. "I concentrated on comparative politics."

Tabitha's statement did nothing to change Keith's expression. "And what is *that*, then?"

"The study of constitutions, political actors, legislatures and associated fields, all of them from an intrastate perspective," she replied again.

"Is this girl talking English?" Keith asked Doug, sitting next to him.

"I think it's academic English. It's an English

no one really understands unless they are a member of their secret order. Like a clan," Doug answered. Keith nodded.

"Look, politics and government is *my* one skill," Tabitha winked at Keith. "At least for my contribution to this discussion—and putting aside the whole *I have a genie wish* thing."

We sat in uneasy silence while they stared at one another. I heard the creak of a chair, and the wheezy breathing of the wereducks, but beyond that? Nothing.

"Would you help us, then?" Scout called to Tabitha from across the room after a few minutes of awkward suspense. "Our world is not your world, but you have knowledge we do not. Would you be willing to help?"

"I'm *here*, aren't I?" Tabitha asked, turning to him.

"No, no," he said as he swung his hand. "What I mean is, would you help us? Act as a…an advisor. Someone that could help teach us about setting up a city government that benefits all the clans. Not just one."

"Move to Elysia?" Tabitha asked, frowning.

"Now just a minute—" Doug said as he bolted up, but Scout stood up with force and held his palm out toward the kelpie, silencing him.

"The Witches' Council could *never* admit when they were not suited toward something," Scout told Doug and the kelpie crossed his arms. "They mowed our rights and our people down and required us to fit within their view of how things should be or suffer death. If this human knows how we could avoid replaying the mistakes our world has made, isn't it worth it to get her help?"

"You're saying we're not suited to run our own world?" Doug snapped, his face contorted with outrage and resentment.

"I'm saying unless we are sincere about what we know and don't know, want and don't want?" Scout frowned, and then took a deep breath, his shoulders slouching slightly as his posture relaxed. With a quieter voice and gentle eyes, he smiled at the kelpie. "Brother, we *could* fail again, and leave ourselves open to the same issues we just faced."

Fear crossed Doug's face, and he nodded suddenly.

Then he sat down.

"I propose we move forward with the hu—" Scout caught himself as he gazed at Tabitha. "With Tabitha's recommendation. All in support of setting up an interim City Council made up of one representative of each clan? That representative must live in Elysia," he added. "All in favor?"

Many hands raised.

"All opposed?"

None.

"The elected interim council has been formed. I presume the clans can choose their members utilizing their own methods to do so," Scout nodded. "On to Elysia's mayor. If you would like to stand for that interim position, please do so now."

Bodies fell into chairs and to the ground so fast that Scout Trout was the only one left standing within two beats of a bat's wing. Even Cama flew from the ceiling to hide in my hair.

The werebear leader called a vote, and he was elected interim mayor, also unanimously.

Scout Trout's first act as mayor was to call a vote to abolish the Witches' Council's rules oppressing all the paranormal world, which passed, unanimously again, with a cheer.

His second act was to get down on one knee and propose to Devana, the huntress witch.

The cheer that went up when she accepted?

It shook the yurt.

CHAPTER 21

WE DIDN'T HAVE MUCH TIME TO CELEBRATE THE engagement of Scout and Devana. Everyone on the grounds prepared for a teleport to Elysia, the new home of paranormals open to all magical creatures (and various humans that could find it). The interim mayor felt it was essential to keep the momentum moving.

"What about the other cities?" I asked Scout while we trudged toward the edge of the Magical Midway.

"I'll reach out to them by cauldron, but they're not exactly cities, Charlotte," Scout said. We halted every once in a while as people presented themselves to congratulate the newly engaged mayor. "I think calling them villages would be a stretch."

"I've never visited," I shrugged.

"Are you sure you're okay with all this?"

"All what?"

"Well, there's a good chance when we fly to Elysia, we aren't going to be embraced as liberators," Scout pointed out. "Your power will be the only thing stopping a fight there."

"I'm all about stopping fights," I told him with a shrug.

Scout looked at me with an expression of real curiosity, and not a small amount of concern. "You know, Charlotte, you look *incredibly* unaffected by all this."

"I'm not *unaffected*," I said defensively, glancing up at the sky. "This just wasn't anything I ever really wanted for myself, you know? When the ancestors chose me in that circle, I accepted the charge to look after the circus, but I don't really expect that's *why* they chose me. I think they picked me because they knew I would end it. Everything happens for a reason, you know?"

"You're not actually *ending* something, Charlotte." Scout and I walked up to the border and I turned to face him. "Well, okay, you are, but that's not the important part of it. You're starting something, for everyone. Paranormal and human alike."

I stared across the stretch of the in-between world and sighed. Gunther had truly done an extraordinary job, and the place was magnificent.

The sun gleamed, and in the distance there was a sparkling lake with silvery fish that jumped. The leaves shimmered on the trees as if he infused them with flecks of gold when he formed them. The air was serene due to the blossoms that flourished everywhere, releasing a gentle perfume of serenity.

I would miss this place. Some girls got a bouquet from their partner.

I got a secret utopia.

"Are you worried about our reception at Elysia?"

"Perhaps I should be, but not really," Scout said after reflecting on it quietly for a few moments. "I gave it some thought, and I think everybody had trouble with the Witches' Council in one way or another."

"You know, there are other members. Of the Council, I mean," I told him. "The three World sisters, they weren't the only ones."

"They were the only members that actively struggled against the community," Scout shrugged. "Rumor has it the others sit in the palace day in and day out, waited on by attendants."

"You don't think they'll put up a fight to keep that?"

"I think the servants would put up more of a fight to get out from under their control. And besides," he grinned. "There are far more servants than Council members. I don't think it will be an issue."

"So, we're going in, putting the Midway down in the middle of the place, and then you want me to extend the Midway's boundaries so I incorporate all of Elysia," I detailed for the final time as I raised my palms. "You're positively sure?"

He nodded. "I can't think of another way to do this. I assume most will side with us, but if the Council hasn't been forthright with those people? Who knows what they'll think is taking place."

It wasn't nearly as grand, or as inhabited, as I expected it to be. I'd been told it was dazzling, crowded, magnificent—and this was anything but.

The buildings had a striking uniformity to them, concrete block homes on street after street. All with the same doors, same windows, same size, and the same design. All five floors tall.

"It's so...*gray*," I told Scout, peering across the small expanse. "Gray buildings on gray streets hemmed in by a gray mist. I mean...*this* is the grand and dazzling Imperatorial City?"

"By day, the city *is* drab at first glance," Gunther strolled up behind us. "But if you study closely, you can see that the buildings shimmer with flecks of silver and white ever so slightly. It's meant to carry the moon into the sun's realm. Gray and white, shimmers and shadows."

"So what happens at night?"

"It glows with bright colors. That's when it's *really* incredible."

"Doesn't that make it hard to sleep?"

"They are asleep now." Gunther gestured out to the nearly empty street. "The city awakens at nightfall."

"That...makes no sense," I said, examining the horizon. "Why operate exactly opposite of everyone else?"

"Partly because it is contrary to most of the world." Samson crept up on us and snaked his body affectionately around my leg. "What better way to keep individuals from being able to operate in the human world than by having the time here run counter to it?"

"No wonder the Witches' Council was always so pale," I told the cat. Samson nodded.

"Charlotte, if you would, could you remove the walls?" Scout asked as he pointed to the twenty foot high border wall just inside the mists.

"Just gone?" I asked him.

"Yep, gone."

"Okay, then," I nodded and squinted at the wall. In a split second, the surrounding wall disappeared.

"There. Much better," Scout smiled. "Shall we head to the palace?"

"What palace?" I asked, perplexed. "All these buildings look completely the same." Ugly, gray, boring, and monotonous. I certainly didn't see *anything* that resembled a palace.

"That one," Gunther pointed.

"How can you tell?"

"It has nine stories," Gunther answered as if it were obvious.

Gunther's face grew thoughtful as Scout and I stepped toward the border of the Magical Midway and drew closer to Elysia. Samson stayed behind, watching Gunther with interest. I turned and looked at them, starled at Gunther's expression. My eyebrow raised.

"It's nothing," he murmured. But he didn't step toward us.

"It looks like something to me."

All of us stopped and stared at Gunther who appeared practically glued to the ground. His eyes were low, his breathing quickened. If he was a human, I'd guess he was having some kind of mild panic attack.

"Gunther?" I stepped toward him, but he held up a hand.

"I know that you and Dad turned me into a full witch," he answered quietly while staring at the ground, his face tense. "I recognize that I likely won't glow, won't light up like a bright bulb. But I have to concede I have an odd…dread. I dread setting foot on that road."

I opened my mouth to speak, but Scout got there first.

"You have just as much right to be here as anyone else, Gunther. Probably even more than most. You always did. We all always did," Scout told him as he turned back and considered my husband…um, boyfriend…Gunther. "Your first step will be the first step in unifying the city and the community. I am privileged to be here to see you take it." He followed the statement with a polite smile.

Scout Trout had come so far since I met him and suspected him of assassinating his brother.

He strode back to Gunther and held out his hand.

Gunther grabbed it and stepped forward while holding his breath. Looking up, he grinned at Scout—then glanced down at his hand in the beefy werebear's. He dropped it like it was on fire and coughed. "I've got it, thank you."

"I'm sorry if I made you uncomfortable," Scout apologized. He tried to hide the grin. "Bears are very physical with one another and we think little about it."

"Well, you got my consent, so no harm no foul."

I rolled my eyes as the three of us began walking.

"What about the rest of the new city council?"

"I felt it was best that just the three of us went

in the city. Gunther is familiar with this place, and I *am* its new mayor," Scout told me. "You, of course, are the equal of a military garrison. Just in case."

"I don't think they'd see me as a garrison so much as an occupying force."

"But you are a garrison," Scout reminded me. "All the clans have agreed that this is what will be. And there is no leader here anymore."

"Think again, bear," Mabel World shouted as she raced into the street to face us.

Alone.

Which, in retrospect, she probably regretted.

"What have you done with my sisters?" Mabel screeched in a tone that could have been recorded and sold for use in audio torture machines. "Just because we have been dumped by Eiggam doesn't mean that we no longer rule here, invaders!"

"Actually, I'm relatively certain that's *literally* what it means," Scout told her without trying to hide his amusement. "You're alone now, Mabel. Your sisters are not to be able to help you, so I recommend that you stand down. We don't want anybody to get hurt here."

"Not even you," Gunther added quietly. I peeked at Gunther in confusion. I had previously extended the Magical Midway energy, and so the restriction on hurting—

Oh. Me.

They were talking about me possibly squashing her like a bug.

"What are you talking about? Where are my sisters?" she demanded again.

"Mercy is hanging out with Gunther's mom. You know, the one Mina killed?" I informed the tired-looking witch. "And Mina's been changed into a cat. I assume she's still working through the shift in her circumstances, so even though cats can be handy, she won't be useful to you."

"*Some* cats are useful," Samson replied. I turned around and noticed my familiar had followed us quietly into the city.

"Thus I am in charge!" she shrieked.

"Yeah, no, you're not," Samson told her with a yawn.

"You are in the vast and powerful Imperatorial City! This is my realm!" she screeched. She lifted two fists above her head and stretched her fingers wide, palms toward us. Bending her elbows briefly, she thrust her hands toward us and puckered up her face intently.

Nothing happened.

She glanced up at her hands momentarily, shock registering on her face. Narrowing her eyes, Mabel bowed her elbows again and propelled her palms toward us more forcefully. "You will perish here!"

Gunther, Scout and I glanced at one another, standing by to perish. Samson laid down on the ground and snapped his tail.

Nothing.

"Maybe we should have brought up that we moved the Magical Midway here, with us. Oh, and that Charlotte expanded the borders of the magic that runs the Midway to precisely match the borders of Impy," Scout explained to her amiably. "Which, by the way, isn't called Impy anymore. The city council has voted to change the name back to Elysia."

"*What* city council? There is *no* city council. There's only the Witches' Council, and we have proclaimed that *you will die!*"

"You're a real competitive sort, are you?" I asked her. "You do remember you can't kill us, anyway, right? Tabitha's wish bound you."

"I would die to see you dead!" Mabel spat. "We

would let *you* live, Scout Trout, but you've aligned yourself with the insurgents!"

"If you kill us, there will be no you, remember? I *really* think since we have a council, have renamed the city, and you *don't* have any friends left, that *we're* actually not the insurgents. You're actually the insurgent," Scout explained to her calmly. "And, frankly, as far as rebels go? I was expecting a lot more of a reception." *Scout* glanced around at the quiet street.

The magical non-shootout at the battleship-colored OK Corral was beginning to attract attention. Mabel's high-decibel shrieking had clearly woken up the inhabitants on either side of the street, and faces were now staring intently out their windows.

"You cannot have the city," Mabel protested.

"We don't want the city," Scout said. "Not the way *you* mean it. We want everyone to have the city, everyone will be able to come here and get educated if they wish. To live here if they want to. Or come here on vacation if they so desire. Yes, we want to take the city from you, but we want to give it back to the people."

Windows were opening so people could hear what Scout was saying.

"If you want to lead the city, Mabel, you are perfectly welcome to run for mayor."

"Mayor? Mayor? Are you daft, bear? This magical city doesn't have a mayor!"

Scout walked up to Mabel slowly and looked down at the woman. Despite all her screeching and hand-waving, she couldn't do anything to stop us.

And as she kept glancing back fearfully at me, I *knew* she knew it. This was over the moment she lifted her hands and couldn't cast against us. Within the magic of the Magical Midway was the seed of the city council's new Golden Rule (inspired by Tabitha and borrowed from humans).

The one thing everyone would have to abide by, enforced by the very magic that animated this place.

Do unto others as you would have them do unto you.

And if you wouldn't take it, you couldn't deal it.

It had worked to stop the Witches' Council. We hoped it would work to stop future Minas.

Doors were opening.

People walked quietly, barefoot, out onto the street.

Mabel looked around at the expression of fascination on the faces of the people she believed to be her subjects. Her incredulity slowly twisted until her face was a mask of rage. "You did this!" she hissed at me.

"Not just me," I told her, smiling. "But I had a hand in it. So did you, actually, that first night you came to my circus and demanded that I bow down to you. You set the wheels in motion for this, Mabel. You and Mercy and Mina."

The witch howled, the expression on her face a mixture of towering hatred and indignation.

"You *are* welcome to stay," Scout told her, reaching out his hand. "But you must live as an equal to everyone else, and you have to live by the rules that everyone agrees on. The past is the past. We will all start new, together."

"We will all live under her thumb, you fool! She could kill any one of us at any moment for any reason!" Mabel shouted at him with clenched teeth. "Are you a complete idiot?"

"Once we settle in here and we've established what we needed to establish magically, Charlotte will be releasing the rest of her ringmaster power into the world," Scout explained. "Yes, she's giving us a start. What we do with that start, though, is entirely up to us."

That brought Mabel up short, and she looked at me like I'd grown another head. "*You* are a complete idiot," she deadpanned.

"Maybe," I shrugged. "Probably a good reason for me not to be in charge of the entire world, then, right?"

Gunther chuckled.

CHAPTER 22

It was doubtless the most anticlimactic coup in the history of revolutions.

"This wasn't *really* a coup," Samson said. He sat in the window on the ninth floor of the palace looking out over the city. "A coup is what Mina World did."

"Have you been talking to Tabitha?" I asked the cat.

"I *know* things," he answered haughtily, his ears leaning forward. A bird in the tree beyond the window looked back at him and trilled. "Tease," he rumbled. Then, standing up in one movement, he hissed loudly. The bird screeched in panic and frantically flew away.

Scout had been right. With Mercy having

defected, Mina a cat, and Mabel…well, Mabel World was never the brightest *or* most skilled *or* wisest of the sisters. We had conquered the three of them for good, it seemed, with a five-minute chat in a street. Those remaining in the new Elysia seemed universally grateful for it.

Once it was apparent that a military occupation would *not* be necessary, I pulled back to the top floor of the palace with Samson. I didn't wish to disproportionately influence what Scout and the council did with the city they now had the duty to oversee.

"You have done well," a dusty shadow whispered from the corner of the palatial suite. I shifted to see Cama and her mother moving toward me.

"I'm glad you approve. I think," I told the shadow goddess.

"I was *speaking* to my offspring," the darkness rasped as it gestured toward the bat. "But I suppose congratulations are in order for you as well, Ringmaster. You got this far without ending the world."

"Gee, thanks for that."

"I have spoken to the other gods," the billowing black smoke told me as Cama flew around her.

"They are satisfied with this conclusion and will not intrude further. We will allow you to continue on the path you have started here."

"*You'll* allow *me*?" I asked, incredulous. "*You'll* allow *me*? You know we only had to do all this because the gods interfered in the first place and exploited us as patsies, right?" I told her, feeling my anger flare. "This was all of us fixing *y'all's* mess."

"Do you *really* wish to arouse the wrath of a god when you have just extinguished a wrath that took *two hundred and fifty years* to work through, child?" the shadow woman inquired. Sparks flashed within her roiling black vapor.

I could feel the tears stinging my eyes at the mere thought that an erroneous word could accidentally set *all this off again*. I willed my eyes dry and my mouth to remain mum.

"Leave her alone," Samson said with a yawn.

"Brother, it took you long enough to—"

Wait.

Brother?

"Silence!" Samson shouted. He bounced off the windowsill. As he arced through the air his frame grew, and grew, and grew. When his paws struck the floor, and he paused in front of the shadow woman, I wasn't gawking at a small, snarky black cat.

I was staring at an over-sized jaguar.

"I realize that with the politics and infighting quelled, you all are in for a span of ennui," Samson growled out. As he exhaled, a rough and threatening sound emitted from his savage face. It was almost like a cat purr—if a cat purr was purred by a freaking dragon.

The shadow did not respond.

"I would propose that you discover other diversions to fill your long days. That you are here at all is troubling. These people won the right to be free of you." The big cat's brilliant golden eyes blazed as he paced, and the sound of his tremendous claws against the concrete floor sounded like blades being honed against a whetstone.

Cama squeaked and shielded behind her mother.

Unflinching, the shadow woman shrugged at the indignant cat. "Quiet yourself, brother," she murmured with a jeer. "I mean your witch no harm."

His witch? I started to wonder who belonged to who, here.

"Then get out," Samson growled low.

"I will go," she answered, leaning down to stare into Samson's eyes. "But I have one further role to perform, and we will see each other once more. Try to control yourself at the appointed time." The goddess looked up at me as she began to vanish. "Come, Cama. Your job is done here."

"Awww, but Mom—"

"Cama!"

"Can I come back and see Charlotte one more time? When you do the thing, you know, that we can't talk about because—"

"Cama!"

"I'll come back when you do that *thing*," Cama squeaked as she flew in whirling circles around her mother and they both started to fade at the same rate. "I'll see you tomorrow, Charlotte! I want to be there when you get your reward! Bye!"

The panther and I stared at one another, and as I peeked into Samson's eyes I could see myself reflected back at me. An expression of bewildered frustration contorted my face as I stood, frozen.

⁓

"Questions?" Samson asked roughly, the peculiar low roar underneath the words.

"No," I squeaked and deliberately stepped backward.

Samson narrowed his eyes and stepped forward.

I quit moving.

"No?" he asked. I swear, the thing looked amused. If something slobbering, menacing, and murderous could also look amused.

"Okay, maybe one," I tried to say, but I couldn't make the words come out in anything other than a tense, froglike croaking. The height and look of the big cat, the natural aura of menace coming from the panther? It was startlingly horrifying.

Cama's mother had *nothing* on Samson's capacity to make you pee your pants with a glance.

Samson rolled his eyes. I guess that gesture of annoyance didn't change based on what form he was in.

"Once I was called the Night Sun," Samson said as he began retreating back to the simple black cat that I had known—but that evidently I had never *truly* known. "As the world changed, I changed my name. Or maybe it evolved, I don't know," the small cat yawned, the dynamic and intimidating voice supplanted by the indifferent, detached tone I was used to.

"Are you the reason for the whole night and day business?"

"Oh, sure, blame me," he said sarcastically. He vaulted back to the windowsill and settled down to gaze out at the city again.

"Okay, if it's not you—"

"No, I mean sure, you *can* blame me," Samson repeated. "You were never going to fix that, but it was good practice for you trying to figure it out."

I fumed, but said nothing.

"You *really* want to say something to me, don't you," Samson observed. He laid on his back and displayed his belly.

"No," I lied, crossing my arms. I didn't want to give the cat the satisfaction of knowing just how hurt I was that he had been lying to me all this time. I also didn't want the cat to turn back into a gigantic panther and rip my throat out. "Whatever. You know, nothing in this place is ever what it seems. It's fine."

"Come on, Astley."

"Really. I'm fine."

"Are not," Samson said, and then he yawned. "Tell me how you really feel."

"Well, I *would*, but you're an enormous,

menacing *panther god*, and you might *rip my throat out* if I make you irritable."

"Right, because it's not like I've had reason to want to do that before," the cat dropped his head off the edge of the windowsill and peered up at me upside down. "Look at me. I'm an adorable kitty cat. Come on. Speak up."

"How could you *not* tell me what you were?" I challenged him angrily, hurt.

"I told you what I was, and you saw it for yourself. I claimed I was a guardian, and you saw the cord," Samson informed me as he flipped over. "It's not my fault you don't read mythology books. You could've guessed it in the first couple of months we met. Besides, does it matter? Am I not simply who I am?"

"But you've been in our family…or, more accurately, *with* our family for over two hundred years!"

"So?"

"How did no one recognize what you were?"

"*None* of you read mythology books?"

I glared at Samson.

"You could have saved yourself when you got captured," I sputtered. I began pacing.

"Well, technically, yes."

I stopped pacing and stared at him. "You put

me through all that for nothing?"

"Charlotte, look around you." Samson gazed back out. "Events happened as they had to develop so you could set things right again."

"You're a god, couldn't *you* have set things right again?"

"That *free will* thing you guys have, that's a *real* pain in the butt sometimes, I'll concede," Samson said.

"Did Ms. Elkins know who you were?" I asked him.

He held up his paws. "She's close to a god in her own right. So probably."

"Wait a minute, what happened to this whole there are no gods thing, you're just higher level beings, it's an expression of convenience and—"

"Oh, no, there *are* gods. You're facing one. But again, does it matter? Am I not simply who I am? Are we not simply who *we* are?"

"I really have a headache," I whined and buried my face in my hands. "I just want to get this over with, get out of here, and save stray animals. That's it. No more gods, no magic, no reading minds, no teleporting circuses."

"That sounds *dreadfully* boring," Samson told me with an eye roll.

"Maybe I'm over*due* for dreadfully boring!"

Samson sneezed a snort. "Sure, okay."

My eyes narrowed. "Why did you say it like that?"

"You'll see."

I waited, but Samson wouldn't say anything more than that.

"Samson, what do you know that I don't?"

"If I *truly* answered that question, you would starve to death sitting there listening to all of it," Samson replied. "Have some faith that *everyone* gets what they warrant in the end."

"Are we at the end?"

"I don't know, *are* we?" Samson asked me.

I chewed my lip not knowing whether to be delighted, or petrified.

"And I have no idea what it means," I told Gunther hours later.

As I related the story, he peeked over at Samson repeatedly, his face astonished. "What I can tell you is I am so *done* with all of this! Done. I thought I would feel sad, but now I just want to get out of Dodge as soon as I can, strip off these powers like a bad fashion choice, and go get some ice cream that wasn't manifested by a genie."

"Charlotte, we've *all* always recognized that Samson was somehow...*different*," Gunther said as he leaned in mildly. "I understand it was doubtless quite a shock to see him in his true form, but—"

"He lied to me," I told Gunther coldly.

"Did not," the cat grumbled from the windowsill.

"And he's still keeping things from me."

"Okay, you've got me there," the cat shrugged.

"When can we go?" I pleaded with Gunther. His face looked sad as he gently gathered me into his arms and kissed the top of my head. "I just want to go home."

I felt like Dorothy at the end of *The Wizard of Oz*. Okay, I wiped out the evil witch for you, liberated Oz, you're all free. Love you all. Happy for you. That said, *when can I get the bloody hell out of this lolly-pop flavored, yellow-bricked dystopian nightmare?*

"Tomorrow, if you like," Scout said stepping in with a wide grin. A grin that decreased as he took in my haggard look, Gunther's concern, and Samson's eye roll. "Everything okay in here?"

"Ask the Night Sun," I pointed.

Scout blanched, his smile dropping off his

face completely as he gawked at Samson in reverence and awe.

"Finally, *someone* that reads a book now and again," Samson muttered. "Relax, bear. After all this, my war god aspect is taking a bit of a vacation. Besides, Tez and I made up years ago."

"*War* god?" I asked, stunned.

"Among other things," Samson nodded.

Scout bowed grandly to Samson.

"I'm so confused," I complained.

"Read a book," Samson countered.

"But not today," Scout said, shifting back toward me. His eyes took a bit to follow, but he finally turned away from Samson. "We've come up with some things we'll need you to do, like link this place with the in-between place—"

"Why?"

"Vacations?"

"Some families are not keen on going into the human world at all, and the place we had will make a nice getaway for them if they need a change of scenery," Gunther explained.

"Expand the land, build more housing. For the most part, it's just city planning and housekeeping stuff," Scout nodded and handed me a list.

I glanced over it and shrugged. "This might

take me an hour at most." I noticed that the Magical Midway would be integrated more fully into the city, but it wouldn't entirely go away. "Do I need to stay until tomorrow, then?"

"Oh," Scout said, looking surprised. "No, I guess not," he said, shifting uncomfortably.

"What?"

"Nothing," the werebear said, clearly meaning the opposite of the words that were coming out of his mouth.

"Scout, *what*?"

"I…we'll miss you, Charlotte." Scout smiled at me. "We owe a lot to you, you and Gunther. Devana and I want you to be here for our wedding, and I had hoped to have some kind of presentation, a key to the city—"

"Oh, dear lord, don't have me create a magic key that unlocks the city!" I told him, horrified.

He laughed. "Symbolic, Charlotte. Just symbolic."

"Right. Sorry," I told him sheepishly. Gunther looked at me concerned.

"Look, I don't think it's a good idea that you have a superpowered being walking around once this is done," I told him. "And honestly, now that this is almost over? I just want to get back to my normal life."

Samson snorted.

"*What* is your issue?" I snapped at the cat.

He turned and stared ominously at me, his eyes narrowing.

"Your life has *changed*, Charlotte Astley," Samson intoned as he leapt off the sill and grew again to the gigantic, menacing panther. Pacing, his golden eyes held me mesmerized as he confronted me. "You will *not* be able to rubber-band back to your old life once you shed this power. This is not like a snake shedding its skin. The universe *knows your name* now."

"Wow," Gunther breathed. "That's sure something."

"I'll say," Scout choked.

"The universe can just *lose* my phone number after this," I told Samson haughtily, even though my insides were quivering like jello. "Because I'm done. Do you hear me? *Done*."

"Do not lose what you have gained," Samson warned, and then he turned and walked out. Screams echoed from the hallway, the sound of feet running, followed by roars.

"You don't think he'd eat people, do you?" Scout asked.

I glared at Scout, but I didn't answer.

CHAPTER 23

THE NEW GOVERNMENT, LIVING QUARTERS, ELYSIA vacation spot—it was all set up with surprising speed. Scout and the city council decreed that Gunther and I would be given ten percent of the Midway's human monetary resources. When we protested, Scout said they needed to be sure we could continue our work with the animal shelter for years to come.

They would split half of the rest between the Midway's inhabitants that wished to go into the mortal world (to honor what I had told them would happen), and they would hold the other half for those that preferred to leave in the future.

Aidan and Kyle would stay in Elysia and

manage the human money and investments for the city council.

"Are you positive you won't come back to Mickwac?" I asked Aidan, crestfallen.

"We talked about it extensively, Charlotte," Aidan said. He reached out and grabbed Kyle's hand. The two men smiled at one another. "This place is far friendlier to us than anywhere in the human world would be. Sure, in some respects, this place is behind."

"In some aspects, it's ahead," Kyle finished for him. "It makes a difference."

It saddened me to hear him say that, but I knew they were right.

"We'll keep them busy," Scout said. He and Devana joined us in a rotunda at the front of the palace. "I'm still trying to convince Kyle to take on the role of police chief. He's intimately familiar with how the humans do things—"

"Which, sometimes, isn't that great," Kyle pointed out.

"So, you'll do it better," Aidan told him, smiling.

"Gunther, will you be going with Charlotte to Mickwac?" Scout asked.

"Where she goes, I go," Gunther said, gazing lovingly at me. I blushed. Scout put his arm around Devana and smiled. "We'll come back for your wedding, of course. My parents, too."

"Your parents are going to Mickwac?" Aidan asked Gunther, surprised.

"With my Uncle Phil and Jeannie, too," I nodded. "It seems kind of crazy, I realize, but I think for the Makepeaces, this place will always hold *terrible* memories. That, and they want to be where we are."

"For the grandchildren, no doubt," Devana said, her mischievous eyes twinkling.

"Gunther and I don't even know whether we're *married* at the moment, so let's slow down, there, huntress," I told her, blushing again.

"Oh, for goodness' sake," Samson mumbled from near my feet.

The entire group jumped back and gawked at the cat.

"*Really?*" he asked, insulted. "We're still doing that?"

"Well, your excellency, you *are* a god," Scout told him.

"So were Maggie and Eiggam, and it didn't stop Romeo here from sticking them in a box," Samson pointed out, staring at Gunther.

"That was different," Gunther told Samson.

"Well, sure, *you* were a god then, too," Samson

agreed. "Now it's just Nervous Nellie over here," he added, waving his paw at me.

"I'm not a Nervous Nellie!" I shouted. "What does that even mean, anyway?"

"It means that you're—"

"Samson, enough," Gunther told the cat quietly. Everyone in the circle stared at Gunther in shock. "Perhaps as a god, tremendous changes do not affect you as much. We are not as immune to the effects of such great upheaval. You should be kinder to Charlotte," Gunther continued, his voice gentle and respectful, but firm. "She has righted the earth, but just because it is now *right* doesn't mean it isn't all *different.*"

"Gunther, you both corrected the world," Devana told him.

"Perhaps she had assistance, it's true," he half-smiled as he winked at Devana. "It is still a little disorienting." I stared at Gunther, who looked neither nervous nor disoriented. "I would just ask that you back off for a bit."

"Wait, a bit?" I repeated and glanced down at the cat. "You're not staying around, are you?"

"What, just waiting to get rid of me?" Samson asked me. Devana and Scout glanced at one another.

"But you're a god!"

"I've always been a god," Samson pointed out.

"But...but...I can't have a panther god of war sleeping on my bed in Mickwac!"

"Why on earth not?"

"Because...because...because *you're a god*!" I said again, hoping that this explained everything. I had consistently assumed that Samson would stay with me just because he had been attached to my family for so long. And then he exploded into all his panther glory. Now that I knew his true nature, though, I wasn't entirely sure I wanted him to. Gods hadn't exactly been reliable, steady companions.

"Oh, stop the dramatics, Charlotte," Samson told me as he jumped up on my shoulder. "I can pick any pillow in the world. Yours are previously broken in, and you're already well-trained."

"*I'm* well-trained?"

"Besides, I think the Avalon Grove could use a new deity," Samson said and he patted me on the head.

It took several hours for us to say our goodbyes and leave. Even though we promised to return for the wedding in two weeks, it felt like a permanent farewell.

"Tabitha and Bob are already at your parents'," Gunther told me. We strolled toward the mist. Samson walked some distance behind us. "Your uncle and Jeannie, too."

"I feel like I should be more sad, more freaked out," I told Gunther. We wandered slowly through the streets of Elysia gazing at everything as we went. People seemed…happy. "I have no circus, most of our friends are staying here. Everything's different."

"Charlotte, you are plenty freaked out," Gunther laughed.

"I am not!"

"You are," he nodded. "Samson's not wrong about your anxiety returning."

"Returning?"

"I think sometimes you don't realize how much you changed since you arrived here," Gunther mused, looking up at the stars that were just beginning to peek out in the dusky sky. "When I met you, you struck me as a girl dropped into a fever dream, just trying to muddle her way through a land she didn't accept."

"Like *Alice in Wonderland* or Dorothy in *The Wizard of Oz*," I murmured, knowing Gunther wouldn't understand the references. He looked over and smiled at me. "They're human stories."

"I had no doubt," Gunther said with a laugh.

"I can't wait to share a lot of these things with you, you know," I told him and caught his hand. He winced at the pain, and I dropped it as quickly as I'd grabbed it. "I'm so sorry, I didn't mean—"

"I know! I know, love, it's fine," Gunther replied, stopping. I stopped beside him and he reached out to gently turned me toward him. "Charlotte, you began this journey as a sheltered girl, protected from all the truths that affected her own life. All the parents, gods, powers, legacies, everything that passed down through time to affect what you would do, every prophecy that dictated who you would be. You defied them *all* to do what you believed to be right."

"I had to," I told him. "I didn't have a choice."

"You had a choice," Gunther disagreed. "You always had an option. That's what I am saying, Charlotte—all of this, all the things that happened, all that we've accomplished. It was all because of your choices. Sometimes, I feel you don't see that—that *you* did this. That you can do anything you set your mind to."

"You're giving me way too much credit—"

"I'm not," Gunther said emphatically, ending the debate.

Samson hurried over to us as if he sensed a pause he could wiggle into. "You should listen to him. Now that that's settled, where is that cat of *yours*?"

"Delilah is with Anna back in Mickwac," Gunther told Samson. We watched a group of witch children clustered around a werewolf, laughing as they ran by us on the street. "Why?"

"Just concern for a fellow feline." Samson spun with his tail up and walked on ahead.

Gunther and I stared after him.

"You don't think…" I trailed off.

"No," Gunther said once, and then paused. Then he shook his head no, but paused again. After a few moments of staring after Samson, he whispered, "He said she was a child. No, it couldn't be."

He turned back to me and we stared at one another.

"We need to get back to Mickwac," he and I both said together, and we took off after the cryptic god-cat toward what was left of the Magical Midway.

～

When my mother helped me through the cauldron, she was excited.

"I think you'll love it," Mom was blurting while she and Dad placed me on the floor and then turned to pull Gunther through. "Tabitha and your Uncle Phil really outdid themselves though, of course, it was really Jeannie that did the heavy lifting."

"What heavy lifting?" I asked her as Gunther's feet hit the floor.

"It is nice to have humans we can trust around," Mom continued. We walked toward the rear porch. "The coven was instrumental in helping to set it all up. Thank goodness we had enough humans to spread the wishes around."

"If you don't like it, though, Charlotte, you must make any changes the old-fashioned way," Dad explained, pushing open the rear door. "We've run out of humans for wishes at this point."

"What on earth are you two *talking* about?" I asked. I stepped onto the back porch.

Then I stopped and stared in shock. Gunther crashed into me with a clang.

My vision or dream or whatever you want to call it.

It was here. The houses in a U around the

shelter, a small carnival in the back. It was all there. As if I closed my eyes, imagined it, and just willed it into existence.

"But…but…how?" I asked in a choked whisper. Walking to the edge of the porch, I scanned the horizon, taking everything in. It was my dream. My dream, my desire, sitting *right there*. "Is it *real*?"

"Do you like it, Charlotte? Do you?" little Anna asked me excitedly, flying in front of my face. "Mama said we get to stay here with you now, and we needed a house, and Uncle Phil and Jeannie will live there and you and Gunther will settle there and—"

"I don't understand," I whispered.

"Your friends got together to wish you a new life, Charlotte," Jeannie said as she stepped next to me. "That house over there is a duplex, and I'll live there with the ghosts. Over there," she pointed, "is your house. Yours and Gunther's. And that?" she pointed to a small carnival-like setup next to the shelter. "That's a small children's fair. It's fenced in so that people coming can bring their pets, take some of the animals in the shelter there to spend time with them—"

"Please, stop," I whispered, holding up my

hand. Jeannie fell silent, and I could feel her concern.

"Are you all right, love?" Gunther asked me quietly, stepping up on the other side of me. As he came closer, Jeannie drifted back.

I could sense frank stares of everyone on the porch, but I didn't care. It was overwhelming.

I turned toward Gunther. I could scarcely see him through my tears.

"Charlotte," Gunther said with more insistence.

"I'm okay, I'm okay, I just…I can't believe they did this," I told him. "I can barely believe it's real."

"I told you." Samson jumped up on the porch railing. "Everyone gets what they deserve in the end."

"Is this what your sister was talking about?" I asked Samson, wiping away the tears that had stained my face.

"This?" Samson laughed. "Oh, no."

"No?" I demanded incredulously.

"This is far too simple for a god," Samson chuckle-hissed as he rubbed against my arm. "Some wood, some metal. Maybe some plumbing if you're lucky. No big deal."

"Hey!" Jeannie protested hotly.

"I'm just saying," Samson said, ignoring

Jeannie. "The goddess of death and rebirth isn't going to build a cottage for you. That's all."

"What's that now?" my mother asked, concerned.

Once I got myself back under control, we sat down with our families and explained everything that had transpired since we left, and Samson parked himself languidly at the center of the outdoor table flicking his tail.

CHAPTER 24

"ARE YOU READY?" JEANNIE ASKED ME. WE STOOD on the ledge of the coven's hidden grotto pool. "Going in the water may not be needed at all, but this is the biggest wish I've ever granted. I'd like to cover all my bases."

"Yeah, no, I understand," I responded. I studied the dark waters and swallowed. The air was humid, and the observers silent. The moon high in the sky beamed down into the cavern and shimmered off the still water.

"What do I do with the lamp once I make the wish? Anything?" Tabitha asked, her tone tinged with a faint, nervous tremor that I'd never picked up from her before. Jeannie answered her, but I didn't hear it over the ringing in my ears.

"It'll be okay," someone spoke to my right. I shuffled restlessly from side to side and then gazed up, struggling to focus on who was talking to me. Gunther. It was Gunther. Of course it was Gunther.

"Right, sure, I know," I murmured distractedly and my eyes slid back to stare at the still water.

I had watched Gunther give up his powers, and he didn't look at all the way I felt right now. I recognized this was the right thing to do, I truly accepted it had to be done, and yet I was more fearful than I assumed I would be.

"Will it hurt?" I asked no one in particular.

"I don't think so," Jeannie answered from someplace behind me.

"You don't *think* so?"

"I've done nothing like this before, Charlotte," Jeannie reminded me anew. "Gunther may be the best person to answer that question, though even his answer may not tell you what you're about to experience. He spent his power. I'm yanking out yours."

I wobbled on my feet a little and gulped.

"Charlotte, you *don't* have to do this," my mother called across the cave. She stood watching me, her face wrapped in concern. "You've done so much already—"

"Mom, do you want grandchildren?" I asked her.

"Grandchildren?" Mom asked, perplexed. "Why, of course, Charlotte, I—"

I cut her off by loudly knocking on my metal shield. The clang echoed off the walls of the cavern. "That shield protects every inch of my body," I told her, looking up. "*Every* inch. Do you follow what I'm saying, Mom?"

"Yes, Charlotte, I understand—"

"Nothing gets in. Nothing gets out. You understand?"

Mom blushed and placed her hand over her mouth, miming the zipping of her lip. Dad stood mute beside her and gripped her more closely. His face was pale.

"Wait a minute, she doesn't pee?" Bob asked me, aghast. When I didn't answer, he leaned down. "How does she pee?" he whispered to Tabitha.

"I don't think peeing is the issue here, Bob," Tabitha whispered back.

"You're dilly-dallying," Samson said to all of us. "We're here, there's the water. Let's get on with this. Delaying it will only make everybody more irritable."

Jeannie's face was solemn when she stepped up to me. "I don't care what the cat says—"

"God," Samson yawned. "Now that we all know, let's give the immortal his due, shall we?"

"Fine, I don't care what *the god* says," Jeannie said with an eye roll. "We do this only when you're ready, Charlotte. You tell me. But all is good to go on my end, and Tabitha's ready to do her part."

I turned to glance at my human friend, and she saluted. Then Tabitha gave me a tired smile. "You *got* this, Astley."

"Right," I said and then exhaled. Leaning down, I took off my shoes and socks and gave them to Gunther. He took two steps back and set them on an outcropping of rock. I wiped my sweaty hands on my pants and tiptoed closer to the edge. "Okay," I mumbled. "I'm ready."

Behind me, Tabitha began reciting a long wish that she and Jeannie had worked on in an attempt to cover every single possible loophole. Almost as soon as she commenced reading, the pool appeared to twinkle as if ghosts swam just beneath the surface of the water.

"Jump now, Charlotte! Now!" Jeannie shouted.

I took a deep breath.

And I plunged into the water.

The water swirled around me as if I had been crammed into the center of the world's biggest washing machine. Lights blinked and sparkly ribbons of what looked like stars sped by me.

My hands, my feet…energy flowed out of them, adding to the ribbons. I could still breathe in the water just the way I could before, but it felt like someone had turned on a tap and was slowly diminishing the oxygen in my body.

Light found crevices, cracks, and flowed out even though the water level was stable. The springs that seeped up pure water from below now looked like light vortexes as the starry ribbons pushed against the flood to get out of the spring any way they could.

It felt like I was down there beneath the water forever.

Just when I felt I couldn't take any more, the water calmed somewhat, the light faded, and a breath drew in water with the oxygen I had formerly pulled from the water just fine. My throat and lungs burned as I began battling to reach the top, alarmed that I would drown myself in the deep water if this kept going.

But I couldn't find the surface.

It was so dark, so deep. The churning had spun me around so many times I didn't recognize which way was up and which way was down. My confusion grew. I flailed harder, positive that this moment could be the end of me.

"Help!" I shrieked, but it came out as a gurgle, absorbed in the dense water's swirl.

Suddenly, a white form appeared before me, moving diagonally. I worked to steady myself, and peered at it, working to get an understanding of what it was. As it kept drifting, I realized it might be floating up, and I imitated its trajectory, paddling wildly in the same direction.

It felt like hours, but a few moments later my head split the surface, and I gasped air into my lungs with the most unladylike of noises. Coughing, I peered around for someone to help me.

Gunther stared, astonished, and bolted into the water. Gasps echoed in my ears as the witnesses stared into the pool in my direction. I bobbed, waiting for Gunther to rescue me.

And I waited.

And I waited.

What the—?

Finally, I swam weakly toward the outcropping of rocks, and Tabitha reached down to lug me out of the water. Rolling over on my back, I settled there and hacked the water I had inhaled out of my lungs. Bob looked down at me with apprehension and moved to turn me to my side, but I waved him off. "I'll be fine," I croaked. "Just give me a minute."

"Are you sure?" Tabitha asked, frowning. I nodded and coughed until I could breathe more comfortably.

"What the hell is with Gunther?" I demanded angrily once I caught my breath sufficiently to give a good, powerful vent to my displeasure. Tabitha helped me sit up, gently, and wrapped big towels around me while I continued shivering. "This wasn't exactly the ideal moment for a swim, you know? Why didn't he help me?"

"Um, Charlotte," Tabitha said, and then bit her lip, gazing back behind her at some sort of commotion. "He had to save…the…um, the baby."

"The what now?" I asked. An infant's wail began ringing off the walls. "*What* baby? Whose baby? A baby what? What the hell are you talking about?"

"You popped up, boss," Bob said, nodding. "And then a *baby* popped up."

"A baby. A *baby* popped up out of the water. Like, a real baby. With me."

"Yeah, I wouldn't have believed it, either, but I swear, you both broke the water at the same time, and I think Gunther was worried the baby would sink," Bob continued. He helped me rise up.

"Oh my gosh, it has Grandma Astley's eyes," I heard Dad say in a strangled whisper. "Gunther, he looks like you!"

"This *obviously* wasn't part of the wish," Jeannie told Uncle Phil. They peered down at Gunther and the baby. "I don't know what went wrong, Phil. There wasn't even an iota of wiggle room anywhere that a baby could wiggle out of! I swear!"

"Calm down, djinn, this wasn't about your wording." Samson strode into the center of the circle. "Let's let the witch that released the world catch her breath first."

Without waiting for an invitation, I clambered to thrust myself off the rock I was leaning on and headed toward the crowd. Tabitha and Bob helped to support me, and I was confident I looked like a drowned gnome. My blue jeans squished uncomfortably as I stepped over to the group huddled around Gunther and the wet baby.

As my parents stepped back so I could peek down, my insides froze in awe, and my head swam with dizziness. The baby looked back up at me with a grin.

The baby from my dream. "Rollie," I whispered.

The baby giggled in reply.

"Your gift," a throaty voice announced from the other side of the cavern.

I looked up to see Cama, Cama's mom, Maggie, and Eiggam staring back at me.

The four bowed and then disappeared.

It was an intense evening, but a peace had descended on the grotto.

I nestled Rollo in my arms. The baby slept sedately, his tiny little hand wrapped securely around my finger. Gunther sat behind me holding me, and I leaned into his warmth.

"It *is* their child, Gunther's and Charlotte's," Samson told Uncle Phil. The ghost peppered him with questions. "As for how, I could tell you, but you wouldn't understand because you're not a god. As for why, because the gods were thankful to Charlotte and Gunther for their assistance and their sacrifices."

"It's what she wanted, but what about what *he*

wanted?" Uncle Phil demanded. "He gave up his power, too. She had that dream thing, but what about—"

"Are you indeed such an idiot that you haven't realized that boy would lie down and die for your niece? It's no wonder you never settled down with any of those women. At least not until you were dead," Samson told him haughtily.

"If you're going to stick around, you and I will have to have a talk about the concept of privacy," Phil told that cat and he glanced toward Jeannie. "You've seen too much, cat."

"We don't even know if we're *married*," I sighed to Gunther. "And suddenly we have a family. We have a *son*, Gunther."

"And he's as beautiful as his mother, as miraculous as his mother," Gunther whispered back. The rest of the people stood around us debating with Samson the hows, whys, and wherefores of what had just taken place.

I didn't need to understand anymore.

I didn't care.

Sitting on a rock in a moonlit grotto I had everything I could have ever wanted.

My baby in my arms, and Gunther's arms around me.

"You think Rollo is short for Roland?" I asked Gunther.

"Your dream didn't tell you?"

"No."

"I think he's Roland Philip Makepeace," Gunther replied.

"That's a beautiful name," I told him, grinning. His statement finally shut Uncle Phil up. "What do you think, little love? Roland Phillip Makepeace work for you?"

The baby burped.

"Charlotte, darling, we should get home," Mom said as she leaned down. "You all need to get in some dry clothes, and we need to take your crib out of the storehouse for Rollie. Oh, and I can cauldron your Aunt June. I expect she has some baby clothes we can use until we can get to the store. Of course, if..."

I tuned Mom out while she immersed herself mentally with a checklist of preparations for the baby that was already here.

CHAPTER 25

"It's fascinating, Charlotte," Fortuna told me two days later, swaying with the baby on the porch swing. The two of us looked out over the Astley Midway. "Their principles and ethics are so simple and yet so sophisticated. I'm picking up a lot from Avalon Grove."

"So you will stay in Mickwac, then?"

"I thought about it," she responded softly. She peered down at Rollie. "But there was something about Rollie that reminded me of…well, me." Glancing up, her eyes looked distressed. "He was kind of a foundling, too, but it took only seconds for you all to know his entire story. Why he came into existence, that he was yours and Gunther's.

He'll grow up knowing where he belongs, enveloped by people who love him."

I frowned. "I know you didn't have the best childhood, but we love you, Fortuna. You have a place where you belong now."

"I do, that's true," she smiled and rose up to wander back and forth slowly. Rollie, the most remarkable child on the entire planet, dozed peacefully in her arms. "But it's not enough—oh, I don't mean to sound ungrateful!" she continued hastily when she saw the hurt on my face. "With Scout's honorarium, I can afford to settle anywhere I choose."

"Where will you go?" I asked.

"Mystic's End," she announced with her back toward me. "It's a small town in Arkansas. Where I was found."

"The place with that big casino and greyhound track?" I asked much more judgmentally than I aimed to. I detested any kind of animal abuse, and we'd received more than one greyhound from that place.

"That's it."

"And with a name like Mystic's End? That just sounds…ominous, Fortuna. Especially for a witch."

"I'm sure it's *just* a name."

"What will you do there?"

"Open up an art gallery, I think," she responded, shifting toward me and grinning. "Or maybe a studio where people can come and make art. I don't know. Something like that. Mostly, though," she said, sitting back down, "I need to experience where I came from. Maybe look for answers. Why I inherited telepathy, why it awakened when I came to the circus. Why...why someone didn't *want* me," she sighed. She glanced down at Rollie in her arms as he began to awaken.

"Have you ever even *been* there?"

"Technically, I suppose I have, but no," she shook her head, and looked up when Gunther stepped out onto the porch.

"Sorry, ladies, just wanted to check and see if anyone was hungry, thirsty, needed a diaper change."

"I am well-fed and well-hydrated, and I don't require a diaper change, Gunther," Fortuna told him with a chuckle. She got up and held the half-slumbering baby out to him. "This young man here, though, might be a tad bit ripe."

He nodded and gently cradled Rollie in his arms, murmuring to the child as the two went back inside.

"How did he know?" Fortuna asked me.

I shrugged. "No idea. He's never been particularly telepathic, but he seems to have some mysterious sixth sense when the baby needs something." The two of us heard Gunther singing to Rollie through the open window of the nursery. "It's kind of hot, if you want to know the truth."

Fortuna laughed.

"Look, I don't want to tell you what to do, but remember, you have a home here with us," I told her, standing up to walk over and sit next to her. She smiled at me and smoothed her light blonde locks from her face. "If it gets to be too much, too upsetting, or you get too lonely, you can always come back here."

"I know that, Charlotte," she nodded.

"I may not be a ringmaster anymore, but I can offer a marvelous life playing with cats and dogs," I joked, nudging her. "And I'm sure Mickwac could use an art studio, too."

"Maybe," she nodded. "For now, though, I think I need to do this. Even if I can't find out who my birth-mother was, I can go learn about the town that I came from."

~

"Delilah!" I hollered as Gunther's familiar raced off the dinner table with an entire chicken thigh in her mouth.

"Oh, let her go," Gunther laughed fondly at the devious, playful cat darting out of the room trailing chicken grease and tomato sauce. "I'll tidy up the mess as soon as we're done with dinner."

"Life was a lot easier with those cats when I could just zap them." I grunted. I picked up the plates and put them in the sink. Running the water, I stared down as it slowly filled up, and shuddered, recalling the long minutes in the washing machine as the air slowly drained from me.

I didn't even recognize when Gunther reached around me to twist off the faucet. "I'll get those later," he said. He swung me toward him.

"I've got—"

"If you think I can't see you stare at water like it's a seething pool of serpents, then you don't think very much of my powers of observation," he declared, placing his hand under my chin and tilting my head up. "It's only been two days, give yourself some time."

Two days. Had it only been two days?

We must be an exceptionally resilient family.

My mother found nearly all of my baby

furniture in the storehouse in record time, with help from Gunther's mom (who could dart in and out of boxes identifying contents faster than anyone could open and search).

Dad put it together along with Gunther, while Roland and Uncle Phil shouted conflicting directions at them. Or, well, they tried to. The four of them looked so haggard that Jeannie lost all restraint and granted a wish for the entire nursery to be set up and done—even though there was no human around to wish for it. I am *pretty* sure she broke some genie rules to do it.

Anna was over at our house most of the time. If she wasn't just gazing at her nephew, she was working with Gerda to practice solidifying enough to be able to hold the baby.

Gunther and I scrambled to adapt to being new parents with capabilities far, far more restricted than we were used to.

"You're right," I told him, nodding and kissing him on his nose the way we used to when we were both armored up. "Okay, you can do the dishes. I think I will go check on the baby."

"Knock knock!" I heard my mother say from the back door. Without awaiting an answer, the deck door lurched open, and she marched inside.

"Mom, the baby's sleeping," I told her, confident she wasn't here to see me.

"Wonderful, I bet I can get him to my house without waking him up, then," she declared as she rushed past me and marched with purpose toward Rollie's room.

"Wait, what?" I said, chasing after her. "You don't have anything over—"

"Stop," my mother said as she pirouetted to face me and held her hand up. "I recall how little time I had to myself when you were born, Charlotte, and any offspring of yours must be up every two hours to complain like clockwork."

"Well, yes, but—"

"You and Gunther have been through a bunch, and I'm sure you haven't had a minute of alone time since you gave up your ringmaster powers," she responded, raising an eyebrow and peering back and forth between us.

"Well, no, but—"

"All of us grandparents talked about it, and we will take care of the baby for the next few hours so the two of you can spend some time reconnecting." Mom whirled on her heel and strode toward the baby's room. I followed her in.

"Mom, I—"

"Quiet, Charlotte, you'll wake the baby," she

hissed. She gathered the sleeping Rollie into her arms and turned around to walk out.

"But Mom, we—"

"Charlotte, lower your voice, please," she whispered more insistently. She tiptoed around me and marched with my son down the hall, through the kitchen, and out the back door.

"Mom!"

Once the door was closed, she turned and glanced at me through the screen. "I'll bring him back at 11:30 p.m.," she whispered. "You two have a good time."

A second later she marched down the steps and was gone.

Gunther and I stared at one another. The silence was deafening.

"So, what do you want to do?" he asked sheepishly.

I blushed.

Gunther walked deliberately toward the kitchen light and reached out to flip it off. The lights from the midway in the back streamed in, and we could hear children giggling. Turning to me, he held out his hand.

I hesitated, staring at it.

He frowned. "Charlotte?"

"Are we married?" I burst out.

"Oh my goodness gracious, are you kidding me?" Samson screeched from the back of the house. He and Delilah raced out and hopped on the kitchen table. "What is *wrong* with you?"

"*Nothing* is wrong with me!" I informed the cat hotly. "We just didn't *properly* get married, it was all knotted up it the ringmaster magic thing, and since we gave that up, did we give up being married, too? I just need to know!"

"Why?" Samson asked, his sneering tone not quite as snide.

"Because it matters!"

"Is this *really* who you choose to spend the rest of your existence with? Seriously?" Delilah asked Gunther.

"Yes," Gunther answered his familiar seriously. "Yes, Charlotte is who I want to spend the rest of this life with. There is no one else in this world or any other world I would rather be with," he advised the snotty little cat gently.

I blushed.

Delilah rolled her eyes. "Can't *you* do something?" she asked Samson. She paced the table. "What's the use of you being a god, or whatever it is you *claim* to be?"

"Watch it, chicken thief," Samson growled at her. "Fine." Samson turned to study at me. "Do you?"

I squinted. "Do I what?"

Samson let out a sequence of four-letter words.

"Do *you*," Samson said, brandishing his paw at me, "want to marry him?"

"Of course I do!"

"Okay, *you* previously said *you* wanted to marry *her*." Samson waved his paw in Gunther's direction. "By the power vested in me by…um…I don't know, *something* vested me with authority, so I'm marrying you. There. You're wed. Congratulations. Happy now?"

I blinked again. "That's it?"

"What do you want, a medal?" Samson asked me.

"A ring would be nice," I confessed to him. "A wedding, maybe."

"You're *hopeless*." The cat spun and strode away, his tail in the air.

"Yeah, *hopeless*," Delilah agreed as she followed him off the table.

The cats jumped up to the window and raced out of the house.

"I assume he was trying to help," Gunther told me while he started poking around in his pocket. He pulled out two gold bands and held them up. "Would these work?"

I gasped. "Where did you get those?"

"My parents," he said as he slipped them both into my palm. "A goldsmith back in Elysia recreated them for me while we were there. They're copies of Mom and Dad's," Gunther smiled a half smile. "I thought it would be a good way to carry on their legacy, you know?"

Gunther got down on one knee and held out his hand for the band. I dropped one into his palm, gazed, and he caught me by the hand before I could pull it away.

"Charlotte, do you agree that you are married to me as of this moment forward? That you agree to be the mother of my child, and the bride that I will work incredibly hard to get a *real* wedding for just as soon as it's convenient?" he asked me earnestly as he held the ring up. I laughed and nodded.

Gunther slipped the gold band on my finger. Standing up, he held out his hand and waited.

"Gunther, do you agree that snide, ridiculous

marriage ceremony we just had performed by a god-cat means we're *actually* married?" Gunther laughed and nodded. I slipped the wedding ring onto his ring finger.

"I love you," my again-husband whispered. He reached down and raised my lips toward his. "You've made me happier than I ever dreamed I'd be, Charlotte."

"I love you, too," I told him, and we kissed. A long, deep, married-person kiss. As we pulled away, we hugged and laughed like giddy, sleep-deprived children.

"Considering everything we've faced, that was actually a pretty appropriate wedding ceremony for the two of us," I told him. I lifted my hand and stared at the gleaming gold band.

"You might be right," Gunther said and glanced down the hall toward the bedroom. Then he looked at his watch. "What do you say, Mrs. Makepeace—ready for our three-hour honeymoon?"

I nodded, gave him a kiss, and we both went through the house shutting and locking all the windows and doors.

And cat doors.

～

I hope you enjoyed the final book in the Magical Midway series *When Curse Comes to Love*! Follow Fortuna Delphi on her new adventures in Mystic's End with Book 1 in the new Mystic's End Mysteries, Mystic Guests!

KEEP UP WITH LEANNE LEEDS

Thanks so much for reading! I hope you liked it! Want to keep up with me?

Visit leanneleeds.com to:

Find all my books…

Sign up for my newsletter…

Like me on Facebook…

Follow me on Twitter…

Follow me on Instagram…

Thanks again for reading!

Leanne Leeds

FIND A TYPO? LET US KNOW!

Typos happen. It's sad, but true.

Though we go over the manuscript multiple times, have editors, have beta readers, and advance readers it's inevitable that determined typos and mistakes sometimes find their way into a published book.

Did you find one? If you did, think about reporting it on leanneleeds.com so we can get it corrected.

www.ingramcontent.com/pod-product-compliance
Lightning Source LLC
Chambersburg PA
CBHW031544240626
47153CB00002B/377